M
Giroux, E. X.
A death for a dreamer

Oct
17

SEP 22 1989 *2-6-91 (27)*

A DEATH FOR A DREAMER

Also by E. X. Giroux

A DEATH FOR A DREAMER

E. X. GIROUX

ST. MARTIN'S PRESS
New York

Library of Congress Cataloging-in-Publication Data

Giroux. E. X.
    A death for a dreamer / E.X. Giroux.
      p.   cm.
    "A Thomas Dunne book."
    ISBN 0–312–02901–2
    I. Title.
PR9199.3.S49D394   1989
813'.54—dc19   89–30123

First Edition
10 9 8 7 6 5 4 3 2 1

This book is for Frank Owen Shannon and our best friend,
Maca's Doxy Rose

A DEATH FOR A DREAMER

CHAPTER 1

The shrill peal of the doorbell pulled Abigail Sanderson from the cozy depths of an armchair, from the circle of heat beamed by an electric fire, and, reluctantly, from the pages of an engrossing mystery novel. Tightening the belt of her robe around her narrow waist, she padded in slippered feet across the sitting room of her flat, into the tiny hall, and peered through the peephole in the door. The bell pealed again and she jumped. That sound, she decided, was not unlike Aggie's strident voice. Then her face brightened. She wasn't looking at Aggie's wrinkled face but could discern the lines of Robby's long head, the sweep of his light-brown hair. That hair was spangled with moisture, and she hurried to unlock the door.

"What on earth brings you out on a night like this, Robby?"

He smiled down at her. "Neither sleet nor storm shall keep me from checking on your precarious health."

She snorted. "Better get that dripping mac off or your own health may not be so robust. Throw it on the chair and come in beside the fire. What's in the brown paper bag?"

"Brandy for the invalid."

"Couldn't you have made that whiskey?"

"The last time I was here you seemed to have an ample supply of double malt. Gone on a drinking spree? Come to think of it, I could do with a tot of whiskey myself." While she curled up in a corner of the sofa, he headed for the liquor cabinet and tried the door. "Since when have you kept this locked?"

"Since Aggie decided demon drink was injurious to my health and not only locked the booze up but secreted the key." She held out the brown bag. "We'll have to settle for brandy, and you'll have to trot out to the kitchen for glasses."

When they had their drinks and Robert Forsythe was stretching his long legs out toward the hearth, she asked, "How goes the barrister business? Miss me?"

"Smooth as silk," he lied. When Sandy was absent from chambers things never ran smoothly. Briefs were mysteriously mislaid, tempers became short, this morning the coffee machine had broken down and Mrs. Sutter, who had taken over Sandy's duties, had been unable to have it repaired. "We hardly know you're gone."

"Liar."

"I'm not here to talk shop. How—"

"Just why *are* you here?"

"I'm trying to tell you. My, but you are testy. What's the diagnosis?"

"According to Aggie I'm in the final stages of galloping pneumonia. According to the doctor she insisted on calling I have a head cold. That woman! Robby, I can see why Aunt Rose sneaked away to spend her declining years in Corfu. The one area of the world where she knew her cook wouldn't follow her. And who gets stuck with Aggie the Terrible but me!"

He regarded his secretary with a blend of amusement and affection. This feuding with Aggie had been going on for as long as he could remember. Which would make it over three decades now. Sandy, once his father's secretary, had acted as mother to him following the death of his own mother when he was a toddler. And, as Sandy had inherited the ancient cook from her aunt, so he had inherited his father's secretary. Aggie treated her mistress as though she was still a child, and, at times, Sandy acted the same way with him. He thought of mentioning this but decided against it. The cold was making Sandy miserable enough. The tip of her long nose was raw and red, the lids of her pale-blue eyes were pinkened, and even her usually smooth gray hair was mussed. He took a sip of his drink, noticed his companion's glass was empty, and tilted the bottle over it. "Where is Aggie this evening?"

"Visiting, thank God. Up conferring with her crony on the third floor. Mary's Aggie's age and looks even more like a witch than my cook does. In fact, I've a hunch they're circling the cauldron right now and Aggie is probably borrowing a cup of toe of newt and eyes of frog—"

"You have that reversed. According to the Bard that's eye of newt and—"

"Damn and blast the Bard! Now, out with it, Robby. You didn't come out on a night like this to watch me blow my nose. What's up?"

Sighing, he put his glass down. Impossible to conceal anything from this lady. She knew him too well. "Very well. I've just come from a session with Aunt Rachel—"

"How is the dear lady?" Miss Sanderson grinned. That dear lady was as much a bane of Robby's existence as Aggie was of hers. "In good health, I trust."

"Flourishing, except her hearing is getting steadily poorer and she refuses to wear a hearing aid. Shouting at her has made my throat as sore as yours probably is."

"Isn't my throat that's sore. Mainly my nose. What's Aunt Rachel's problem this time? Going to sue someone?"

"This isn't my aunt's problem. At least, it wasn't originally." Forsythe refreshed his own glass. "Belongs to a friend of hers who now lives in California. After listening to Aunt Rachel raving on and shouting questions at her I finally rang up her friend. Luckily Miss Coralund's hearing is excellent. Incidentally, Sandy, she told me the sun is shining in San Diego and the temperature is—"

"And we're having rain, rain, rain. Haven't seen the sun in so long I'm beginning to wonder if it's still up there. But forget the weather report." Over the rim of her glass she regarded him suspiciously. "This problem of Miss—"

"Coralund. Agnes Coralund."

"This problem wouldn't have anything to do with the gentle art of murder, would it?"

"Why do you ask that?"

"Your hobby—"

"*Our* hobby."

"*Your* hobby seems to embroil us in nothing but murder. Why can't you stick to defending criminals, not rooting them out?"

"Methinks the lady doth protest too much. I've noticed that Miss Abigail Sanderson, despite her protestations, finds detection as fascinating as I do." His secretary's mouth snapped open and he held up a hand. "Hear me out. I assure you this is a minor matter and has no possible connection to crime. Miss Coralund simply wishes me to act as her proxy to settle a dispute among the trustees of a home for the aged that she set up and endowed—"

"Whoa! Back up. And top up my glass while you do it."

He tended to the brandy bottle. "This home for the aged has been in existence for over twenty years, and this is the first time the trustees haven't been able to work out difficulties without appealing to Miss Coralund. It appears for any motion to pass, all the trustees, four in number, must agree. In the event of an impasse the decision is Miss Coralund's."

Miss Sanderson sneezed and dabbed gingerly at her nose. "Then why doesn't she hop a jet and come herself?"

"She happens to be about Aunt Rachel's age. Eightyish. Reluctant to travel."

Miss Sanderson's pale eyes fixed shrewdly on Forsythe. "And you're reluctant to act as proxy and are hoping to send me instead."

"For your own good. I know how strained relations get when you're shut up with Aggie for any length of time. A type of cabin fever—"

"Where is this home located?"

"A nice quiet town in the Midlands. Be a great place for you to convalesce. Get you away from Aggie and give you something to occupy your mind. All expenses paid, of course. Unless you're too ill."

"I was thinking of coming back to chambers soon anyway," she muttered. "Self-defense. But tell me this. What's the dispute about? Staff, renovations, a building extension?"

"Dogs."

"*Dogs?*"

He grinned and drained his glass. "I told you it was a minor matter. A few days in a pleasant town and if you do run into a snag I'll be on call. What do you say?"

She took her time, lighting a cigarette, taking a sip of brandy. Finally she shook her head. "No."

"Your reason?"

"I'm not leaving London, driving to a town in the Midlands, to mediate an argument about *dogs*."

"It was only a thought, Sandy." He got to his feet. "I could use a bit of a break myself. No, don't get up. I'll see myself out."

He hadn't reached the hall when the outer door opened and Aggie put in an appearance. The cook must be near his aunt Rachel's age, but the years hadn't made her frail or mild. She was built like a miniature wrestler and had a chin like an outcropping of granite. Her tiny eyes swept coldly over him. "Good evening, Mr. Forsythe," she grated, her tone indicating there was nothing good about the evening. "Been upsetting Miss Abigail, have you?" She lunged past him, one hand clutching a wicker basket. "Told you no visitors, Miss Abigail. You in the state you are."

"Back so soon, Aggie?" Miss Sanderson asked acidly. "What's in the basket? Eye of newt and toes of frog?"

After dropping the basket, the cook clapped a hand over her employer's forehead. "Running a temperature, you are. Turn my back for a few minutes and you start sickening yourself."

"Will you cut it out! You treat me as though I'm still in nappies. Aggie, I'm an adult and have been for a long time."

"Got taller but I swear you'll never grow up. What's this? Drink and filthy cigarettes!" Aggie jerked the cigarette from Miss Sanderson's fingers, butted it, swept up the brandy bottle and the glass, and marched into the kitchen.

By this time Forsythe, making no effort to hide a grin, had pulled on his raincoat and was making for the door. Miss Sanderson trotted up behind him and grabbed his arm. "Is that offer still open?"

"Changed your mind?"

"Had it changed for me." She grinned up at him. "You can carry on in chambers while I go, as fast as I can, to the dogs."

CHAPTER 2

Early afternoon in the Midlands was as gray and wet and, if possible, even more cheerless than London had been. The window that Miss Sanderson was peering through was half obscured with pelting rain. Not that she minded. The view from that window was hardly a morale booster. The street below might once have been graveled but now it was a sea of mud. Across it a group of shabby wooden buildings huddled under a sign stating that was the home of Coralund Textiles. The carpark held only a few cars and one old man wandering disconsolately around carrying a broom. What the broom was in aid of she hadn't the faintest idea.

"Is the entire town like this?" she asked the man at her side.

"Not quite as sordid as this." He wiped a circle clear with a hand the size of a ham. "This is, or was, the industrial area, and you can't expect much beauty here. When I got you settled in at the Fiddle and Bow you must have noticed the high street. Buildings are pretty old but some of them have been tarted up. Hope you weren't counting on one of the picturebook towns the tourists love."

What she'd been counting on, Miss Sanderson had no idea. It certainly hadn't been a place like this one. As for buildings having been tarted up, the inn certainly didn't qualify. It was built of the same grimy brick as the building they were now in. "Was?" she asked. "Is the textile mill shut down?"

"It's still operating but there've been massive layoffs. It's the main industry supporting this place, and the economy here is bad and going to be worse."

"I suppose that will affect the entire district. Is it going to hit your inn too?"

He shook his head. "Hard to say but offhand I'd say no. The Fiddle depends mainly on its pub to keep going. Don't rent out many rooms or serve too many meals. And I notice people on the dole always seem to have enough money to drink."

She glanced up at him. Harry Moore, proprietor of the local inn and trustee for the home for the aged, was a massive man. Tall and with the build of an athlete who hadn't run to paunch and blubber. He had rugged features, a mop of salt-and-pepper hair, and an engaging smile. She'd liked him at sight, but as for his inn . . . she could see why the rooms and dining room weren't in demand. Harry had given her an effusive welcome, a quick introduction to Mrs. Moore, and taken her up to the room that was reserved for her. It was clean, and that was its only good point. Harry had pointed at a few logs arranged on the grate of the fireplace and warned her not to try a fire. The chimney, he explained, smoked badly. He assured her if she felt the cold he could bring up an electric heater later.

"Right now," she said firmly. "Before I meet the other trustees I'd like to freshen up."

"Bathroom and lav at the end of the hall. While you powder your nose I'll lug that heater up. Notice you have a cold."

The bathroom proved to be even colder than her room. Before they left the inn he offered lunch, which she

promptly refused. "Not much appetite," she explained.
She hadn't, but the contents of the plates being carried
from the kitchen had destroyed any she might have had.
So, chilled and lunchless, she had driven Harry to the
Guild Hall. Before her MG slithered through mud to its
door, Harry managed to get on a first-name basis, admire
her car, and give her the names of the other trustees. "The
other members of what Hilary used to call the Gang," he
told her. "Hilary Coralund and two men—Sean Ackerson
and Leroy Dorf."

Now, turning away from the dismal view, Miss Sanderson asked, "Does the mill belong to Hilary or to Agnes
Coralund?"

"Neither. Agnes sold it when she settled up Jamie's estate. The new owners kept the name on. As for Hilary,
she's only a distant connection of the wealthy Coralunds.
Lost her parents young, and Agnes's dad and stepmother
raised her."

Miss Sanderson shivered. "Is there no heat in this
building?"

"There's an ancient furnace but it doesn't do much above
the main floor. Doubt it's even lit today. Better keep your
coat on."

Having no intention of removing that coat, Miss Sanderson glanced around the room. It was a joyless place.
Dull brown wainscoting rose to a discolored ceiling, and
the only furnishings was a long table that looked as though
it had come from a kitchen with five chairs ranged around
it. One chair was at the head of the table, three down one
side, a lone chair on the other. Some preparations seemed
to have been made. In front of each chair were ranged a
water glass, a pad of paper, a pencil. In the middle of the
table was an empty water jug and a gavel. At the far end
of the room a number of framed photographs were out-
lined against the wainscoting. Noticing her glance, Harry
took her elbow and led her down the room. "May be

interested in looking at these. Before and after pictures of the home. This was taken when Agnes and Jamie and Hilary still lived there. This other one was taken last year."

Although the house was the same in both pictures, there were notable differences. In the one taken when the family were still in residence, the house, an eighteenth-century manor, looked homey and cheerful. In the recent picture it looked exactly what it was now, a bleak and rather forbidding institution. "It's changed," she told her companion.

"Bound to. The grounds are pretty neglected now. Higgins does what he can but hasn't time for flower borders and so on. This grove of limes"—a big finger touched the glass—"had to have them chopped down. We hated to but they were old and getting rotten. Have a look at this other picture, Abigail. The lady you're representing is in it and the rest of the Gang. See if you can spot me."

She put a finger on a hulking young man in the back row. "You haven't changed much, Harry."

He chuckled. "Take a closer look. Thirty years makes a lot of difference. I've put on weight and started to gray and got wrinkles. Now, there's Agnes and Hilary and here's Jamie, right beside me."

She took a closer look. The photograph had obviously been taken at the rear of the manor house. Sitting on a bench was a middle-aged woman flanked by two girls. One of the girls had a dark youthful prettiness, the other had a fair beauty. Beside the dark pretty girl sat a pudgy young man. He looked as though he were the type who should be smiling, but his round face was serious and his eyes somber. Behind them stood four young men, all of them laughing, their arms around each other's shoulders.

"Which girl is Hilary Coralund?"

"The fair one. The older lady is Agnes and the brunette is Joanne Parker, or Joanne Drew as she was then. That plump chap beside her is Andrew Parker. Joanne and Andy married and he's the vicar here now." His finger moved again and he said in rather a hushed voice, "Last time we were all together. Good thing Agnes had this photo taken. These are the other trustees. Sean Ackerman and Lee Dorf."

Sean and Lee were both tall and slim and fair. So was the young man beside Harry Moore. But where the trustees were merely good-looking, Jamie Coralund possessed a masculine version of Hilary's beauty. Her eyes fastened on that face, she asked, "Is . . . was Jamie Agnes's son?"

"Brother, or rather half brother. Edmund Coralund married twice. His first wife was Agnes's mother, his second Jamie's. Big age difference. Agnes was twenty-five years older than Jamie."

Feeling a vague sadness, she asked, "He died young?"

"I've no idea whether he's alive or dead." Abruptly Harry swung away and strode back to the window. "That photo was taken on his twenty-fifth birthday. The same night Jamie disappeared—"

"Disappeared?"

"Went away and never came back. Left Hilary practically standing at the altar. They were to have been married the following week. Hey, here comes the rest of the Gang. All tucked into Sean's new car."

Joining him, Miss Sanderson peered down. A sleek Jaguar was pulling up behind her MG. "Now, that's a *car*, Harry."

"Bet your boots that's a car." He grinned down at her. "Sean's the only one of us who can afford something like that."

Harry had already mentioned Sean's antique shop and Miss Sanderson remarked, "Despite the recession the antique business must be booming."

"No idea. But his uncle left him a tidy bit. Lucky dog!"

"Speaking of dogs—"

"You'll have your fill of that subject soon enough. Ah, here they are."

Raindrops spangled the hair of the blond woman and one of the men and starred the bald pate of the other. They pulled off raincoats and, as Harry Moore made first-name introductions, Miss Sanderson frankly stared at the woman. I'm being rude, she thought, but couldn't help herself. Hilary Coralund appeared to have been frozen in time. Only a more mature hairstyle distinguished her from the lovely girl in the photo that had been taken thirty years before. Her figure, displayed in a rose sweater and heather tweed skirt, was as slender and supple and curvaceous, and the face, framed in pale-blond hair, retained the cameo loveliness of the one in the picture.

The bald man hadn't been as fortunate. The thick fair hair of the pictured Sean Ackerson had retreated, leaving a white fringe and bushy sideburns, and the slim body had thickened with a melon-shaped paunch. Even the expensive suit couldn't disguise that bulge.

Across the width of the room, Leroy Dorf looked much the same, and Miss Sanderson recognized him immediately by a flattened nose that looked as though it had been broken and set badly. His hair, parted on the left side and falling in a swoop over part of his brow, was still fairish and thick but as he moved to take her hand she noticed that hair was speckled with gray and his fine skin was cobwebbed with wrinkles.

Miss Sanderson sneezed and Hilary said with quick concern, "You look ill and this place is cold as a tomb. Harry, couldn't you have arranged for some heat?"

Harry shrugged heavy shoulders. "You know the furnace won't heat this floor. I did suggest buying a heater and was voted down." He looked pointedly at Dorf.

Dorf colored faintly. "Good idea, but you didn't suggest where the funds were to come from."

"Well, we'll simply have to tough it out," Hilary said. She turned to Miss Sanderson. "Good of you to come with what looks like a bad cold. Are you a friend of Agnes's?"

"I first heard the name yesterday. But Robby—he's my employer—has an elderly aunt to whom Miss Coralund appealed for help."

"Robby . . . that would be Robert Forsythe. You are both quite famous. Don't look so surprised, Abigail. Even in this backwater we do get London newspapers. But I hardly would have thought private detectives would be interested in our little problem."

"We're not detectives, private or otherwise. Robby's a barrister and I'm his secretary. The cases he's solved have simply been the result of blundering into situations where crimes have occurred."

Hilary fingered her single strand of pearls and light flashed from a diamond solitaire on her engagement finger. Miss Sanderson wondered if this was the ring with which Jamie Coralund had plighted his troth. Curiosity stirred and she fought it down. Jamie's disappearance had no bearing on why she was there. Best to let sleeping dogs lie. Following that thought, she said, "About this dog problem."

"Ah, that world-shaking decision." Ackerman blotted moisture from his white sideburns with an immaculate handkerchief.

Harry glared at him. "Make fun if you want, Sean, but this is important to those poor old people at the home."

"Especially to one in particular, eh? Let's sit down. I'm damp and half frozen but at least we can get off our feet." Taking Miss Sanderson's arm, he led her toward the table. "You have the place of honor, Abigail, at the head of the table. You're to be referee in our dog fight."

As Miss Sanderson took her place the others selected chairs. Hilary took a chair between Ackerman and Dorf, Harry circled the table and sank down on the lone chair facing them. Ah, Miss Sanderson thought, the pros and cons and, judging from the number of dogs she'd noticed at the inn, it looked as though the innkeeper was the pro.

Hilary's lavender eyes flickered toward Miss Sanderson. "It would be simpler if you *were* a friend of Agnes's. At least you'd know about the home. I haven't the least idea where to begin. Do you know *anything* about the home?"

"All I know is that it's for aged people. And, of course, you four are the trustees and are failing to agree on something concerning canines."

The other woman looked at her male companions, and Dorf said abruptly, "We have to fill her in on some of the background."

Hilary nodded and waved a hand at the photos on the wall behind Miss Sanderson. "I suppose it all began the day that group photo was taken. The house and the textile mill were left to Jamie by his father, Uncle Edmund. Agnes had already been provided for in her mother's will. Uncle Edmund's first wife was wealthy, in fact she had a great deal more than the Coralunds ever had. But Agnes had always considered the manor house her home and I . . . Jamie and I were to have been married the following week, and I'd assumed we'd make our home there too. But during the party—it was Jamie's birthday—he announced out of the blue that he'd decided to sell the mill and use the money to turn the house into a home for indigent aged and endow it." Hilary's mouth set. "All because of Nanny Balfour."

Harry was fishing a battered cigar case from a sagging pocket and Miss Sanderson glanced hopefully at him. She was longing for a cigarette but there wasn't an ashtray in sight.

"Must you?" Ackerman snapped. "You know we all loathe smoking."

"I notice Abigail takes an occasional cigarette. Would you like to put this to a vote too?" After pushing himself up, Harry slid back a panel in the wainscoting and extracted an ashtray. He put it down at Miss Sanderson's elbow. She noticed it had the name of his inn emblazoned across the glass bottom. "Feel free," he told her.

"As a former footballer," Dorf said icily, "one would expect better judgment from you. Smoking shortens your wind as well as your life."

"Stow it," Harry said. "It's my life and my wind."

"And you force us to breathe the same air—"

"I said to stow it!"

Dorf mumbled but subsided. Conscious of three hostile pairs of eyes on her movements, Miss Sanderson pulled out her cigarette pack. She wondered if by smoking the cons would decide she was already siding with the pro. Blimey, she thought, behave naturally. She accepted a light from Harry, took a deep drag, and promptly broke into a storm of coughing.

"See," Dorf said smugly.

"My cold," she sputtered. "Not the smoke."

Dorf raised a brow. "No doubt your lungs have been ruined."

Miss Sanderson was in control once more. "Shall we continue? I believe you mentioned a Nanny Balfour."

"Dear old Nanny," Ackerson said. "Still in residence at the home although she must be nearly a hundred—"

"Ninety-seven," Hilary corrected. "Jamie was devoted to her. Aunt Marion was a delicate woman and became an invalid shortly after his birth. Nanny raised him. In many ways she was more a mother to him than his own."

Ackerson nodded his bald head. "The day of the party Jamie told us that although he would provide for his aging nurse, he'd been thinking about other old people not as fortunate as Nanny. In a way, this rather ruined the celebration. Lee, Harry, and I couldn't have cared less what Jamie did with the manor house, but Agnes and Hilary were livid—"

"You're exaggerating," Hilary told him. "Agnes may have been livid but I was merely upset. After all, the manor was the only home I could remember. When Uncle Edmund and Aunt Marion took me in I was less than three. And Lee cared too. Didn't you?"

Dorf pushed the hair back from his brow. His deep-set eyes, Miss Sanderson noted, looked incredibly weary. "Not as much as you did. I lived in that house for only a few years after my dad's death."

Miss Sanderson glanced around the table. "Did all of you live in the manor house?"

The innkeeper shook his head. "Not Sean or I. Sean lived with his mother in town and I was at the inn with my dad and mom. But when we were kids we spent most of our time at the manor."

The secretary swiveled around to look at the group photo. "What about the other members of the Gang? The vicar and his wife?"

Hilary lifted a delicate brow and Harry explained. "Before you arrived I showed Abigail the picture of the party." He turned toward Miss Sanderson. "The Gang consisted of only five members, Jamie and us. Joanne and Andy were similar ages and lived in town but they never . . ."

"Belonged," Hilary finished crisply. "They trailed along behind us, and Joanne was mad about Jamie and Andy was mad about Joanne." She straightened slender shoulders. "We're going far afield, Abigail. To complete the details and make them as short as possible . . . That night Jamie left. The reason for this is no mystery, he wrote me a letter, and none of this has any bearing on what's happening now—"

"It most certainly does," Dorf said explosively. "If Jamie hadn't told us his plans for the mill and the manor Agnes would never have got all of us in this mess."

"Calm down," Harry told him. "We know the past has a bearing on the present but no use in getting upset again."

He butted his cigar and continued, "To try to make that long story short, Abigail, Agnes was shattered when her brother left. For a time none of us could believe it. In his letter to Hilary Jamie said he'd only be away for a short time, a few weeks, and so we waited for him to return. Time passed and a year after his disappearance Agnes decided she couldn't stand being in the manor any longer. She packed and took off to London to stay in the Coralund flat that Jamie and Lee had used for a time. She waited until seven years had passed and she could have Jamie legally declared dead. When his estate was in her hands she immediately turned the house over for a home for the aged and used the rest of the funds to endow it. Then she left England and went to New York. She didn't care for the city and eventually she made her home in California." He stared down at his big hands resting on the table. "We haven't seen Jamie for thirty years and Agnes . . . I suppose it's about twenty-three—"

"More like twenty-two," Ackerson said.

Miss Sanderson was tempted to have another cigarette but decided against it. "And you were appointed trustees before Miss Coralund left England, I suppose."

"That's right," Harry told her. "In those seven years Lee and Sean and I had come drifting back to this town and Hilary had never left it. Agnes was generous and let Hilary stay on at the manor until it was turned into a nursing home. Then she signed over a cottage she owned in town to Hilary. We were right on the spot and all of us had been involved with Jamie so Agnes asked if we would look after the home."

Ackerson tugged his vest down over his paunch. "If I'd had any idea what I was getting into I'd have turned Agnes down cold."

"No, you wouldn't have," Harry told him. "You thought as much of Jamie as the rest of us. We all do it for Jamie's memory."

"Don't say that," Hilary cried. "You make it sound as though he's . . . as though he's dead."

"Face it, darling." Ackerson took both her hands in his. "Jamie *is* dead. If he wasn't he'd have kept his promise and returned."

She wrenched her hands free. "Jamie is *alive*. I know it. I feel it here." One slender hand pressed against her breast. "Perhaps he was hurt and has amnesia but some day he'll remember and then he'll come back to me. Lee, you agree, don't you?"

"Well . . ."

Rather brutally, Harry Moore said, "For once I agree with Sean. No man in his right mind is going to stay away from what Jamie had. Money, that house, you waiting to marry him."

"He was going to give away the house and most of the money," Dorf said flatly.

"It was only a whim," Hilary said. "Jamie would have changed his mind. I know I could have talked him out—"

"For God's sake!" Shoving back his chair, Ackerson lunged from the table. "Why do we always come back to this? Every time we get together it's nothing but Jamie Jamie Jamie! It's been thirty years, and it's still as though he'd never left."

Time to act as referee, Miss Sanderson decided. She reached for the gavel and tapped the table sharply. "Sit down, Sean. Now, does all this have a bearing on dogs?"

For a moment all were silent, and then Harry threw back his head and laughed. "Not the slightest. What we've been working up to or what I *think* we've been working up to is this. The endowment fund established by Agnes Coralund over twenty years ago can no longer cover expenses for the home. At the time it was ample but with inflation and so on it's downright pitiful now, and to keep the place running takes a lot of time and effort."

"I take your meaning," Miss Sanderson said. "How do you manage?"

"With one hell of a lot of difficulty. The vicar and his wife usually put on a fête in the spring for us and then there're charity teas, tag days—"

"To say nothing of bake sales, white elephant sales," Hilary said. "The women's groups are more than supportive. Which reminds me—" She pushed back her sleeve and consulted a tiny watch. "I've a meeting with the Church Guild in a little over an hour. Hoping to persuade the ladies to provide materials for our handicraft room at the home."

Miss Sanderson's ready curiosity stirred again. "Wouldn't it be better to appeal to the government? Have their health service take over the home?"

"No." Color rose in Hilary's fair cheeks. "This is *Jamie's* home. It bears his name."

"Besides," Harry said, "they might close it down, transport the old folks to another place. These are *our* people. They deserve to live out their lives here."

Hilary cleared her throat and turned to Dorf. "Now, Abigail, Lee will fill you in on our dog problem."

Miss Sanderson was rather glad that Lee Dorf had been singled out. The others appeared quite emotional. He said tersely, "Does William Perkins and Sons Limited ring a bell, Abigail?" She shook her head. "What about Perky Puppy Puffs?"

"That name does. I've seen the commercials. Charming puppies gobbling bowls of dog food."

"Good. Have you heard of William Perkins's brainwave?"

"I'm afraid not."

Dorf grimaced. "I think William must be reaching his dotage. Too bad his sons don't have him declared incapable. William obviously dotes on dogs, and apparently he was following all that mumbo jumbo about pets working marvels with old people—"

"Hardly mumbo jumbo," Harry interrupted. "Psychologists have proved that pets have a beneficial effect on aging, lonely people."

Ackerson shook his head until his sideburns bounced. "Only made an educated guess, Harry."

"*Proved*," the innkeeper repeated. "Carry on, Lee."

"If you will allow me to. Harry heard about this insane idea from a chap who works in the office of the Perkins's firm—"

This time Miss Sanderson interrupted. "What idea?"

Dorf sighed but struggled manfully on. "Mr. Perkins decided he would donate a puppy to any aged person who wanted one. Not only that but the puppies would be spayed or neutered and he would provide food for them for a year. Without bothering to consult any of the other trustees, Harry fired off a letter asking Mr. Perkins to consider the Coralund Home as a pilot project. Only after an agreement had been reached did Harry bother to tell us. Hilary and Sean and I were lukewarm to the plan, but Harry argued and bullied and finally we agreed to select four patients and allow them to have puppies."

Dorf paused to catch his breath and Ackerson growled, "I wasn't lukewarm. From the beginning I was strongly opposed to the whole hare-brained scheme. It was you and Hilary who talked me around. I wasn't against a few pets, but we could have given them canaries or goldfish."

In his turn Harry growled, "Ever tried cuddling a fish or bird?"

Ackerson swung on the big man. "Be honest, Harry. You're nuts about dogs. Got mutts all over the inn. Wonder the health department hasn't stepped in." Jerking his blazing eyes from the innkeeper, Ackerson turned them on Miss Sanderson. "Harry's main concern is Maggie Murphy. Maggie tended bar for years at the Fiddle and Bow. She

may be tucked up in the home now, but once she was quite
a girl. Heard rumors she more than drew beer for Harry's
dad—"

"Keep your bloody mouth off Maggie and my dad!"

"Boys," Hilary chided. "What will Abigail think of you?
Sean, you apologize this instant!"

"All I did was repeat what I heard," Ackerson said sul-
lenly. "Okay. Sorry, Harry. No business to repeat gossip."

Hilary took over. "We selected Maggie as one of the
people to have pups because in the last year she started to
go downhill at an awful rate. Maggie had always been so
alert and lively that Nurse Daley and Dr. Falkner were
worried about her. And, in six months, the puppy seems
to have brought her back."

"Bet your boots it has," Harry agreed. "Lass is bright
and jolly and taking an interest again. And look at old Josh
Pitts. Regular demon he was and then he got his dog. The
staff say he's some easier to handle now."

"The dogs don't seem to have made much difference to
the other two," Dorf pointed out. "Miss Allingham is as
cantankerous as ever and—"

"Early days yet," Harry said. "Give it time."

"That's something we don't have much of," Dorf told
him. "Mr. Perkins put a deadline on this project and time's
running out. Either we decide to continue or cancel it."

"You'll take those dogs away from those old folks over
my dead body," the innkeeper said flatly.

Ackerson straightened his tie. "That might be arranged."

Hilary smiled at Miss Sanderson. "Are you beginning to
understand our problem?"

Miss Sanderson had been doodling on the pad of paper.
She realized she'd drawn a sketch that looked remarkably
like a dachshund. "Well, I've gathered the problem is
whether to keep the dogs or have them removed from the
home. I take it the precarious financial condition of the

home has a bearing on it. I also assume we have three trustees against—Sean, Lee, and Hilary. One trustee for —Harry."

"By George, I think she has it," Ackerson murmured.

"And it wasn't that easy," she told him dryly. "However, I fail to see how keeping four dogs on will be a financial drain. After all, they do have food laid on for them."

"For a year." Hilary sighed. "After that, we'll have to provide food. And dogs must have other care too. There'll be vet bills and the dogs will have to be exercised. We'll have to hire someone for the animals' care. The staff are overworked now and claim, quite rightly, walking dogs is not their job."

Dorf raised his tired eyes. "While the pups were being housebroken the staff threatened to walk out en masse. Messes all over the place. Their owners are unable to cope with that sort of thing. Abigail, it's been hell."

"The dogs are housebroken now," Harry said.

Tired eyes turned on the innkeeper. "Would you call Tiny housebroken?"

"Well . . . Tiny is a mite slow. He'll come around."

Putting down the pencil, Miss Sanderson said brightly, "Looking at this objectively, I can't see anything that can't be worked out. Surely there are volunteers connected with the home who could take turns exercising the dogs."

"The town has been most supportive," Hilary said. "Many of the merchants are too. A butcher allows us a percentage of our meat at wholesale prices, and Gaines Bakery donates all its day-old bread—"

"Feeding the poor old devils stale bread," Harry broke in.

"The bread is not stale, Harry, and it's used mainly for toast and puddings anyway. But to get back to volunteers, Abigail. We have a number of people who work very hard for the home on charity drives, and also some of the women read to the patients and ferry them around in their cars.

A couple of them supervise the handicrafts, but we can't locate a single one willing to be a dog handler."

Ackerson grinned. "For that I don't blame them. I notice even our canine fancier here hasn't volunteered."

"Lack of time, not willingness," Harry retorted. "I can't leave all the work at the inn for my poor wife to handle."

Miss Sanderson had been doodling again and an animal vaguely resembling a collie had joined the dachshund. "But surely with only four dogs . . ."

"You still don't understand," Dorf told her. "We wouldn't have appealed to Agnes Coralund for that, or dragged you down here if it were only the dogs there at present. But Mr. Perkins's offer is for *every* patient, if they wish, to have a puppy. Those four dogs are only the vanguard of a mob."

"Blimey!" The pencil fell from Miss Sanderson's hand. "How many patients are there?"

"At present thirty-four. Which leaves thirty to claim pups."

"Don't paint such a black picture, Lee," Harry said staunchly. "A lot of the old folks don't like dogs, some can't be bothered. There's no way we'll have thirty-four dogs."

"Damn right!" Ackerson said. "We'd have to boot out the patients and turn the place into a kennel."

The trustees fell into glum silence. Harry and Ackerson were exchanging hostile looks, Hilary was gazing at the photos behind Miss Sanderson, Dorf stared down at his folded hands. Miss Sanderson printed a line of letters under the dog doodling. Without glancing up, she said, "You seem to be the canine specialist, Harry. How many people do you think will ask for dogs?"

He mulled this over, his heavy chin balanced on one hand. "Maybe . . . about fifteen. Mind, that's only a guess."

"*Nineteen* dogs." Ackerson moaned.

"I think you now grasp the situation," Hilary told the secretary. "You can see how impossible it is, and I'm certain

you will side with Sean and Lee and me. Would you like
to give us your decision now?"

"No way!" Harry was on his feet. "Abigail's only been in
town for a few hours. She hasn't even seen the home yet!"

"Harry's right," Dorf said. "Sit down, old boy. Time's
short, but before Abigail makes up her mind she must
have a clear picture."

Hilary Coralund's lovely head bent in agreement. "I've
been hasty. Yes, you must see the home, Abigail, talk with
the staff and the patients. I'd go with you myself but"—
she consulted the tiny watch again—"I simply haven't a
spare moment this afternoon."

Miss Sanderson felt as exhausted as Dorf's eyes looked.
"No problem. I'd prefer to take that on tomorrow."

"Colds are so hard on one," Hilary sympathized. "But
I'm afraid I shan't be free tomorrow either. I have to put
finishing touches on the preparations for flag day."

"Surely that isn't slated until next week," Dorf said.

"It's early this year, Lee. The day after tomorrow." Hilary rose and smoothed down her skirt and coats were re-
trieved. As Dorf held Hilary's for her, she added, "But
one of the others will be able to escort you. Sean?"

"I'd be happy to but it happens to be my clerk's day off.
Sorry, Abigail."

Dorf settled his own coat on his wide shoulders. "I won't
be available either. My assistant is off with the flu. Guess
that leaves you, Harry."

"Not me, it doesn't. I have to run over to Pendleton to
pick up liquor supplies. A lot cheaper than having them
delivered. Now, the day after . . ."

"This must be settled as soon as possible." Hilary but-
toned her raincoat and picked up an umbrella. "I could
telephone and alert Nurse Daley. Abigail, would you
mind making your way up alone? Harry can give you
directions."

Miss Sanderson agreed and Hilary said, "I'll try to break

away at noon and we can have lunch at the home. You'll find the food rather good."

"The food's swill," Harry announced.

Swill he should be an expert at, Miss Sanderson thought, if the food coming from the kitchen of the Fiddle and Bow was an example. Dorf was opening the door when Harry told Miss Sanderson, "Come to think of it, tomorrow might be a good day at that. Better get up there early. Say around nine."

Swinging around, Ackerson snarled, "What have you been up to now?"

"Just thought with the TV crew being there and all—"

"The *what?*" Ackerson howled.

"The boys filming the commercial for Perky Puppy Puffs."

Dorf and Hilary were forcefully restraining the antiques dealer. Around Ackerson's shoulder, Hilary thrust a flushed face. "They can't film *anything*. We haven't given consent."

"*I* did," Harry said smugly. "Soon as my chum in Mr. Perkins's office rang up I said sure, come ahead."

Ackerson stopped struggling. His voice was as cold and deadly as his expression. "You'd better ring him right back and tell him no dice. They can't use a commercial until they get *all* our names on the dotted line."

"No harm in them shooting it, Sean. It's Mr. Perkins's money, not ours."

"Harry, Harry," Hilary scolded. "You simply must stop doing these things on your own."

Dorf released Ackerson's arm and stepped back. "One moment. Harry, is there any money involved in this? For the home I mean."

The innkeeper rubbed his heavy jaw. "Never thought to ask. But, yes, there'd have to be something."

Pulling down his vest, Ackerson asked. "Why didn't you bring this up in the discussion we just had?"

Harry flushed and shuffled his feet. "Well . . ."

"Because you damn well knew we'd veto it! That's why."

Dorf touched Ackerson's arm. "Look, Sean, maybe it isn't a bad idea. We can really use some extra funds."

Ackerson's face was as red as the innkeeper's. "Sure, we could. But to get those funds there'd be strings attached, I bet. Right, Harry?"

"We'd have to okay the entire project," Harry mumbled.

"See what I mean? Okaying the project means we get another swarm of lousy mutts. Dogs all over the place to feed and look after. End up costing us money we don't even have." Ackerson glared at Harry. "One other point that's driving me bonkers. Why in God's name did you let Josh have a dog that size? This whole business is mad but the maddest part is letting a Great Dane into a home for the aged."

The innkeeper was now thoroughly at bay. He glanced at Miss Sanderson, avoided looking directly at the other trustees, and finally said, "Old Josh had always wanted a Great Dane and—"

"What Josh wants, Josh gets. What Maggie wants, she gets. I'll tell you what you're not getting. That bloody project!"

"Calm down, Sean," Hilary said. "No real harm's been done. As you said the commercial can't be used without our consent. Let them go ahead and film it. Harry, have you bothered to tell the staff about it?"

"Sure," the innkeeper mumbled. "Seemed quite set up about it too."

Dorf's lips relaxed in a smile. "Probably imagining they'll see themselves on television."

"Come along, boys," Hilary said. "Abigail, we'll see you tomorrow. Do take care of that cold."

As the door swung closed behind them, the innkeeper beamed down at his companion. "Don't you go listening

to them, Abigail. Never had pets of their own. Did you
ever have a dog?"

"No. But the aunt who raised me once had a poodle I
was fond of."

"After you visit the home I think you'll see my side." He
patted her shoulder. "You must be chilled. Tell you what,
when we get back to the Fiddle I'll lug up another heater
and stick it in the bathroom. There's a down comforter I
can spare too. Can't have you getting sick."

A bribe? She wandered back to have a last look at the
photograph of the ill-fated birthday party. Her eyes followed the row of young men in tennis clothing, their faces
smiling, their arms affectionately looped around each other's shoulders. She wondered what had happened to Jamie
Coralund, why he had left, why he never had returned.

The innkeeper called, "Aren't you taking your notes
with you?"

"Notes? Oh, I was only doodling. Tear it up."

He looked down at the pad. "Say, you can really draw.
Look at the cute little dogs. What's this you printed?"

"Something that occurred to me when you were shouting
at Sean."

He chuckled. "Hey, this is pretty good! You make it up?"

"It's a quotation, Harry."

He read aloud, " 'Who sleepeth with dogges, shal rise
with fleas.' " He ripped the page off the pad. "Mind if I
keep it?"

"It's yours. But why?"

"Figure, sooner or later, I can use it as ammunition to
fire at Sean."

It was her turn to chuckle. "Sounds more like something Sean could fire at *you*. But I take it you aren't bosom
buddies."

"Couldn't stand each other when we were boys and sure
in hell can't now."

Her finger touched the metal picture frame. "What about Lee?"

"We rub along but have never been close."

"Yet you belonged to the same gang."

"That was Hilary's name for it. Only thing Lee and Sean and I ever had in common were Hilary and Jamie. It was like this." He moved over to the clouded window and made two dots on the glass. Around them, at spaced intervals, he placed three more. "Jamie and Hilary were . . ." Obviously he was searching for words. "They were suns. Golden and beautiful, you see. The rest of us were like plain old planets. Three common people and two young gods." He swung around and grinned. "I'm no hand at words. Have to talk to Lee for pretty words. At one time he wanted to be a writer. Guess he tried pretty hard but never really made it. If Agnes hadn't got him that job as librarian before she left England I don't know how he'd have made out."

Curiosity stirred again and this time Miss Sanderson indulged it. "How do you feel about Agnes Coralund?"

He thought for a moment. "She was old enough to be our mother. Cold and aloof woman. Only person she had a weak spot for was Jamie. She was fair though. Didn't take a pound of Jamie's estate for herself. Used it all to see his last wish was honored and set up the home."

"Hilary said she was raised in the manor. Did Agnes feel anything for her?"

He paused to think again. "As far as I could see . . . no. I had the feeling after Jamie lit out his sister blamed Hilary."

"Why?"

"A silly row Jamie and Hilary had the day of the party. About the gift Hilary gave Jamie." Harry's expression softened. "Agnes was dead wrong. If ever an angel walked this earth, it's Hilary. We all loved Jamie but Hilary . . ."

"You're very fond of her."

"More than fond, Abigail. We're mad about her. Have been from the time we were youngsters and will be until the day we die."

Miss Sanderson had a fleeting thought of Mrs. Harry Moore, a small, harried-looking woman with bitter lines scoring her mouth. "You did marry," she pointed out.

Taking her arm, he steered her out of the gloomy room. As they made their way down the steep staircase, he muttered, "Common folk don't marry gods, Abigail. They only worship them."

CHAPTER 3

As Miss Sanderson pointed the hood of the green MG toward the Coralund Home for the Aged she gaily hummed a tune. She was feeling better than she had for the past fortnight. The weather helped. For once it wasn't teeming rain, and at times a few sunbeams managed to poke their way through the clouds. She had also enjoyed a surprisingly good night. Harry Moore had not only brought up a heater for the bathroom but also offered a down duvet and a blessed bottle of double malt. After a hot bath and three aspirin washed down with a generous tot of scotch, she had slept like a baby. Her host had also delivered a breakfast tray with stern admonishments that she must eat every scrap. She did manage to nibble a slice of cold toast and a few forkfuls of scrambled eggs.

She spotted the gateposts Harry had told her about and swung the little car between them and up a driveway that led straight as an arrow to a parking area in front of the manor. Stepping out of the car, she gazed up at the gray stone building. At that moment the sun fought clear of a cloudbank and beamed a warm light across the façade. The place looked more cheerful than it had in the photograph she'd seen in the Guild Hall.

She trotted up shallow steps to imposing double doors. On the left-hand door a bronze plate announced this was indeed the James Hareford Coralund Home for the Aged. On the other door a notice was tacked telling visitors to walk in. She did and found herself in a spacious foyer. What it had once looked like she had no idea but now it resembled the admittance office of a hospital. It smelled like one too. Several doors opened from it, but the desk was deserted and no one was in sight. She strolled toward the desk and was stretching a hand out for the bell when the door behind the desk swung open and a chunky young woman in a spotless white nylon uniform and a pert cap popped out. Miss Sanderson asked, "Nurse Daley?"

"Yes. You must be Miss Sanderson. Miss Coralund asked me to show you around. I suppose you'll be wanting to meet the patients who have received dogs." She lowered her voice. "Miss Sanderson, don't get the idea I'm trying to interfere with your decision. I assure you I'm fond of pets. I once had a Boston bull and right now I have a pussy waiting for me at home but—" Breaking off, she looked past Miss Sanderson. "Another problem, Mrs. Blecker?"

Another woman had approached soundlessly. This one was stout rather than chunky, older than the nurse, and her uniform was pale pink. She jerked a nod at Miss Sanderson. "I'm afraid so. Eddie Lowell just rang up from the butcher shop and tells me that old van of his has broken down again and he won't be able to deliver my order until tomorrow at the earliest."

"Oh, dear! How do you stand for today?"

"Lunch is all right. There's ham left from yesterday and I'm going to heat it up with rice and peas, but there's not a scrap of meat for dinner. And I promised the patients roast chicken. You know how they look forward to chicken."

The nurse rubbed her brow. "They'll have to settle for

something else. You could make up some of that nice mac-
aroni and cheese—"

"Nurse Daley, I served that for lunch yesterday. If I give
it to them tonight they'll fuss something awful."

"I suppose so." The nurse sighed heavily. "I'll phone
around and see if someone will pick up the order. For now
you relax and concentrate on lunch. Better give them an
extra-special dessert just in case."

The cook's jaw set. "Already made up bread-and-butter
pudding. Not many of them like it but there's only so much
a body can do with the provisions I get."

"You work wonders," the nurse soothed. "Now, run
along and don't worry." She watched the cook waddling
down a hall and smiled ruefully at Miss Sanderson. "One
crisis after the other. Now, what was I saying . . ."

"You were not going to interfere."

"And I'm not. But I must tell you this. In a place like
this four dogs are difficult to handle, but if any more
dogs are brought here I'll be forced to give my notice.
I won't say another word, Miss Sanderson. I'm afraid I
must get on the phone about that ruddy meat order, but
I'll find someone to—Flossie. Do you have a few spare
minutes?"

Flossie looked to be in her late teens, had a bad case of
acne, and was wearing a blue-and-white striped uniform.
She shook her head. "Mrs. Rome is at it again, nurse. I
gotta get up and change her bed."

"Again? I've told you not to let her have so much tea.
Her bladder simply can't handle it. Never mind. Send
down Rose or Cathy."

"They're already down, Nurse. Lucky things are in the
sun room with the TV crew. Sure wish I was. But I gotta
go or Mrs. Rome is gonna be howling her head off."

"Be sure she doesn't get more liquid until lunch,"
Nurse Daley called after the aide. She rubbed her brow
again.

Miss Sanderson took pity on the beleagured woman. "If
you could point me in the right direction . . ."

"Of course. Sorry, Miss Sanderson, things are in a tur-
moil this morning. You'll find the patients you want to
speak with in the sun room."

Directions to the sun room were given and Miss Sanderson walked briskly along one hall, made a right turn into
another. It was warm and she loosened her coat and removed her muffler. Like the foyer, these halls bore no
evidence of once-gracious living. The walls were painted
battleship gray and a matching linoleum covered the floors.
Not exactly cheerful but the place was spotlessly clean.
Despite her problems, Nurse Daley seemed to run a mighty
tidy home.

The hall ended in another set of double doors. When
she swung a panel open she found the sun room deserved
its name. Sunlight was beaming through glass, and a line
of elderly people—one man and three women—were
peacefully seated against the windows. The remainder of
the room was a scene of hectic activity. Lines snaked across
the floor, cameras were being set up by a couple of bored-
looking men in jeans and sweatshirts, three younger men
huddled in a group near the door, and a couple of teenage
girls in blue-and-white stripes were in hot pursuit of what
appeared to be a dozen dogs.

Stopping short, Miss Sanderson counted. She'd been
in error. Only three dogs were racing about among the
equipment. A Great Dane, tongue lolling out, led the
pack with a cocker spaniel and a corgi frisking along
behind.

One of the young men shouted, "Call your dogs! Stop
that big brute and the others will quiet down."

The old man banged one of his canes against the floor
and shouted back. "Tiny's big but he ain't no brute. Just
full of piss and vinegar that boy is. Come on, Tiny, come
to Josh."

The Great Dane stopped in midbound, shook an enormous head, and loped over to his master. The other dogs slowed. One of the girls managed to scoop up the spaniel, the other grabbed the corgi. They were returned to their owners. A big woman with a mass of dyed red curls hugged the spaniel to a generous bosom billowing with lace and strands of multicolored beads. The corgi was deposited on the lap of a thin old lady with shrewd eyes behind steel-rimmed glasses and with a twisted, sour mouth. Miss Sanderson looked for the fourth dog and spotted it. An object the same color and roughly a similar shape as a slug oozed over the lap of the third old woman. In this case there was a remarkable resemblance between mistress and pet.

Miss Sanderson took a couple of steps into the room and the young man who had shouted turned in her direction. He wore jeans too, but his were designer ones and they were topped by a natty cashmere pullover. In one hand he clutched a clipboard and he inclined his head, complete with blow-dried hair, in her direction. His glasses were outsized and rimmed with horn. As he stepped closer she caught a whiff of a pungent and doubtless expensive aftershave lotion. On the narrow cashmere chest a boldly lettered button said "Hi! I'm Ted!"

"Hi!" she said brightly. "I'm Abigail."

"Ah, the lady Harry Moore told me to expect. Allow me to introduce myself. I'm Ted Wimers, PR department, in charge of filming this project." He waved a commanding hand. "Come over here, men, and meet Miss Sanderson. This lady is representing Miss Agnes Coralund."

Apparently the cameramen didn't classify as men. They continued with their work while the other young men moved smartly to Ted's side. Except for the colors of their sweaters—cashmere, of course—they could have been Ted's clones. Her nose told her they even used the same aftershave lotion, but Ted was obviously in command and made introductions all around. Buttons clinging to cashmere chests announced that one clone was Doug, the other Larry. They gave Miss Sanderson sincere smiles and warm handshakes. Buttering her up? She soon decided they were.

"You must understand," Ted told her earnestly, "that we have no actual stake in your decision on Mr. Perkins's generous offer. We merely do our job, which is in the publicity area, but we're positive, and I say this sincerely, that after you've witnessed this touching little film you will throw your weight firmly behind Project Giftdog—"

"Giftdog?" murmured a bemused Miss Sanderson.

One of the nonmen decided to enter the conversation. The cameraman in the green sweatshirt pointed at the Great Dane and called, "Should be called Gifthorse."

Ted ignored this comment. "The name was suggested by Mr. Perkins. An amazing old gentleman, a true humanitarian, of course. Wishing to share with others in delight and reward from pets. Did you know, Miss Sanderson, that Mr. Perkins has *eight* dogs of his own and—"

"Hear his mutts are kept in a *kennel*," the other cameraman contributed.

This time Ted swung around. "Do your jobs and keep out of this!" He turned back to Miss Sanderson and treated her to another glittering smile. "Please take the chair by the door and make yourself comfy. We'll chat when this film is in the can. I promise you'll find it interesting."

She took the chair and shrugged off her coat to "make herself comfy." Ted and Doug and Larry swung into action.

"Camera one?" Larry said smartly.

"Ready, *mein führer*," Green sweatshirt said.

"Camera two?"

The other cameraman merely raised a languid hand.

"Cameras ready," Larry told Ted.

Stepping in front of the waiting senior citizens, Ted addressed them in a soothing voice. "The purpose of this filming is to show your delight in and appreciation of your pets. We'll take each of you in turn. All we wish you to do is hold a package of Perky Puppy Puffs in your right hand and place your left hand lovingly on your pet's head. And then you simply ad-lib. Understand?"

Josh Pitts banged a cane on the floor. "What's this ad-lib stuff—"

"All that means, Josh, is—"

"Mr. Pitts to you, sonny."

"Mr. Pitts, you simply say whatever comes into your head. About your pet and how he thrives on Perky Puppy Puffs. We'll start with you and then Mrs. Murphy—"

"*Miss* Murphy," the red-haired woman boomed.

"Then it will be Miss Murphy's turn and then Miss Allingham—" He beamed a smile at the corgi lady with the shrewd eyes and glasses. "And I did get your name right. Mrs. Safrin will be last."

Three of the oldsters jerked their heads and Mrs. Safrin looked sluggishly off into space. Ted lifted a hand and Larry and Doug moved to flank him. "Okay, men, let's go. Larry, mikes, and Doug, packages."

While Larry scurried to pin the tiny mikes into position, Doug trotted around pressing packages of puppy food into hands. As Larry bent over Miss Murphy, she gave a shriek and clutched at her bulging bosom. "Why, you *naughty* thing!"

Josh chortled. "Giving our Maggie a feeling up, are you, sonny?"

One of the aides, this a plump little thing shaped like a dumpling, told Josh, "Now, you watch that mouth, Josh. Nurse Daley is going to hear about this."

He stretched a gnarled hand toward her chest. "Better watch your own bleeding mouth, Rose, or I'm gonna give you a taste of what sonny boy gave Maggie."

A smiling face poked around camera one. "Way to go, Pops!"

Ted took a sterner view. "Mr. Pitts, I must have your word that you won't swear in this interview."

"You got it," Josh promised.

"Now." Ted looked from one wrinkled face to the next. "Any questions?"

"I have one." The corgi lady's shrewd eyes fastened on him. "Do we get paid for this?"

"The usual fee, Miss Allingham."

"What about residuals?"

"We'll discuss that later. All ready, Mr. Pitts. Hold up the package so the viewers will be able to see the label. That's fine. Put your other hand on your pet's head. Right." He raised his arm. "When my arm falls, Mr. Pitts, start talking."

Josh sat like a statue, holding the package in one hand, his other resting on Tiny's massive head. Ted's arm fell and Josh smirked into the camera and bayed, "This is my dog. Name of Tiny. Mr. Perkins give him to me and he's a good dog. Only trouble with Tiny is that he suffers something horrible with what the vet calls flat-u-lence. Sitting right in the lounge with me the other night and Tiny sneaked out a couple nearly choked us all up. Blame it on this stuff." He waved the package of dog food. "No better than hog slop. Course it's free and maybe I shouldn't complain, but what this dog needs is good red eating meat—"

"Cut!" Ted shouted. He glared at the old man. "You promised!"

"Kept my promise. Didn't cuss once. And you told me to say what come into my head, and that's what I did. May be old but I don't lie. That bleeding food makes Tiny fart something fierce."

Doug and Larry rushed over to Ted and they conferred in whispers. With a noticeable effort Ted regained control, and his hornrims swung toward Maggie Murphy. In low, controlled tones he told her, "Perhaps, Miss Murphy, before you go on camera we should rehearse your segment." He flipped a hand at the cameras. "You can stand down."

Neither cameraman seemed bored any longer. Wearing wide smiles they ambled out from behind their cameras and fixed hopeful eyes on the former barmaid. Maggie, her bosom heaving, held up the package of dog food, and the other hand yanked at her spaniel's silky ear.

"Relax, Miss Murphy," Ted told her. "Now, just say what you had planned."

"My dog," she said shrilly, "is named Poopsie and he's the sweetest thing you've ever seen. Can't tell you how fond I am of him. Makes me happy just seeing him when I get up in the morning. Mr. Perkins must be a nice gentleman to do this for us, and he even sends 'round food for Poopsie. This is the stuff and it's called Pesky Poopy Paps—"

"Miss Murphy," Ted interrupted. "You're doing fine, but that is Perky Puppy Puffs. Would you try it again."

The package dipped but she soldiered on. "This is Poppy Puffy Pips—"

"Let's take a break," Ted said hoarsely. "Men, gather 'round."

The three men returned to a position near Miss Sanderson, but this time they ignored her. Doug patted Ted's cashmere shoulder. "Take it easy, old man. It's simply finding the right approach."

"They're hopeless," Ted said. "It isn't working."

"Perhaps," Larry suggested, "Miss Allingham and Mrs. what's-her-name will do better."

"Face it. We can't let any of them ad-lib. God only knows what they'll say. Miss Allingham may start raving on about residuals. We can't let them open their mouths."

"And that could be the key," Doug said. "What if we just film them sitting there with their pets and use a voice-over?"

"Hmm." Ted adjusted his hornrims. "Bang some ideas off."

For a moment they were deep in thought and Miss Sanderson found she was leaning forward. Then Larry adjusted his own hornrims. "Doug's on to something, Ted. We could use two shots. Kind of before and after. First shot taken without the dogs, black and white, kind of gloomy. Then we use full color, lots of light, the dogs, all the people smiling and happy—"

"Hold that thought!" Ted cried. "Doug?"

"Great idea! Second shot we pile dog food packages in a pyramid between Mr. Pitts's chair and Miss Murphy's. And instead of using a voice-over, we use music. Let the pictures and music speak for themselves."

"Better and better! Music? Something nostalgic. A tear-jerker."

"We got a winner, Ted," Larry enthused. "Go over big with Mr. Perkins. Music . . ." He paused for a moment and then started to warble, "Buddy, my buddy, nobody quite so true." He banged his clipboard against Ted's upper arm. "How about that?"

Ted winced and said flatly, "Won't do. Have you forgotten about Buddy Buster Bites? Want to give free advertising to the bloody competition?"

Larry argued his point. "With that pile of packages we'll have visual product identification."

"What we'll have," Ted told him icily, "is a bunch of

stupid idiots humming 'Buddy.' Strain those little minds of yours and come up with something."

The other two were obviously straining. Then Doug snapped his fingers. "A hymn might do it."

"Right," Larry said wildly. "What about 'Nearer My God to Thee'?"

"Migawd," Ted raged. "Have you lost your mind?"

"Hardly be tactful, Larry," Doug explained. "Considering the ages of the group we're working with."

Miss Sanderson was trying to cough, blow her nose, and stifle a laugh simultaneously. She missed the next few words. When she was able to concentrate she found that Ted was now patting both his men's shoulders. "The idea is a good one. We'll go with it and decide on the music later. Let's get this done."

In a remarkably short time it was done. Dogs, restrained by the young aides, were banished to a corner, Perky Puppy Puffs packages were plucked from four hands, the cameramen returned to position, and the first shot was prepared. Lights were lowered, the oldsters looked unsmilingly into the camera as though contemplating mass suicide, and Ted and his clones looked pleased.

The next shot started out as promisingly. For this one the lights went up, the dogs were dragged back to their owners, Larry unpacked dog food from a carton, and Doug piled it into a neat pyramid.

"Lovely!" Ted praised. "Now, folks, all you have to do is look happy. Smile!"

Four mouths stretched into fixed smiles. Then Miss Allingham's smile wavered, she felt under her corgi, and shrieked, "Rose! Cleo has tinkled all over my lap again! I'm soaked clear through!"

Ted broke. He roared, "To *hell* with Cleo! Sit there and smile until we get this bloody pic—"

"Watch that cussing, sonny," Josh roared back.

The cameramen seemed to be having hysterics. Tiny, who had been sniffing at the dog food, suddenly rose, turned, and cocked one long hind leg over the pyramid. With splendid insouciance, Tiny tinkled all over Perky Puppy Puffs.

In the resulting tumult Miss Sanderson made good her escape from Project Giftdog.

CHAPTER 4

After a vain search for a member of the staff to show her around, Miss Sanderson retreated to the patients' lounge, where she joined an elderly man and two women whose eyes were glued on the television screen. A game show was in progress. Miss Sanderson selected a chair in a corner and picked up a newspaper. It proved to be three days old, so she tossed it aside and tried to interest herself in her surroundings.

In this room an effort had been made to introduce color and cheer. Chintz hung at the long windows and an assortment of chairs and sofas had been covered with pink imitation leather. A number of bouquets of artificial flowers dotted the tables, and she wondered if they had been fashioned in the handicraft room.

Deciding she had better do some research, she canvassed her companions, during a commercial break, on their reactions to having a puppy. The women seemed more interested in the ads than the question but the old man told her bluntly, "Couldn't pay me to have one of the dirty things. Hate dogs!"

After that, conversation languished and Miss Sanderson settled back, staring unseeingly up at the ceiling. After a

time her eyes focused and she decided this was one part
of the home that had been left in its original state. Nymphs
and cupids disported amid wreaths of flowers. The colors
were dim and some of the gilt had flaked away, but it still
had a type of faded charm. Her reverie was interrupted
by a feminine voice. "Ah, here you are, Abigail. I've been
looking all over for you."

Hilary had walked into the room, and against the gray
wall her beauty was startling. She wore the tweed skirt
topped with an ivory silk shirt. There was a glimmer of
lustrous pearls at her throat and a gold bangle on one
slender wrist. The patients lost their interest in television
and smiled at her. She smiled back and greeted each by
name. A gong, close at hand, resounded and she said,
"Lunch." With amazing speed the patients bolted past her,
and Miss Sanderson pulled herself up. "How are preparations for flag day coming?"

"As well as can be expected. Still frightfully muddled
but we should be able to sort it out this afternoon. How
was the TV session? When I arrived the crew were packing
equipment in their van. I stopped to invite them to stay
for lunch but they seemed in a rush. The chap is charge
was quite surly. Was he decent to you?"

"Most cordial."

"Did you find it interesting?"

"Fascinating. Never seen anything like it before."

"Do come and have lunch, Abigail. Sean and Lee managed to get here and they're waiting for us. No, not that
way. Down this hall. We converted the dining room into
a type of cafeteria to make it easier on the staff. Of course
some of the patients can't handle trays, and there has to
be an aide on duty to bring their meals to them."

"Nurse Daley appears most efficient."

"She's a perfect jewel. I've no idea how we'd get on
without her." Hilary brushed back a strand of shining hair.

"The woman we had before her didn't work out. Threw up her hands and walked out barely a month after she was hired. Right in here, Abigail."

Odors of food rushed from the doorway. The room was crowded, and from a table close to one of the windows Ackerson was waving at them. Hilary waved back and led the way to a long counter against the far wall where they took places at the end of a line. Mrs. Blecker, wearing a starched apron over pink nylon, presided behind the counter, spooning food onto plates for them. Miss Sanderson filled a cup with steaming tea and accepted a helping of lettuce and tomato salad but waved away rice and ham and a dish of pudding.

"Appetite off?" Hilary asked.

"Colds do that," Miss Sanderson told her.

Silently she admitted a cold had never done that before, but since she'd set foot in this town her generally hearty appetite had deserted her. Trailing after Hilary, she crossed the floor, skirting tables. She nearly bumped into Flossie, who was carrying two trays, and the aide gave her a nod of recognition. By the time they reached the window table both men were on their feet. Dorf held a chair for Miss Sanderson and Ackerson gallantly seated Hilary.

"Take a look at our local celebrities," Ackerson said. "Stardom seems to have gone to their heads."

The four stars of Project Giftdog were seated at a table with an admiring group of patients gathered around them. Maggie's wide face was as brightly colored as her curls and Josh was banging a cane on the floor. Maggie, Josh, and Miss Allingham seemed to be all talking at the same time, but Mrs. Safrin's gray head was drooping over her plate. None of the dogs was in evidence.

"Modern young fellers," Josh was baying, "ain't worth their salt. Get all riled up and go to pieces over nothing. Know what that Ted called my Tiny?" He glanced around the circle of attentive faces. "Up and called him a 'rotten son of a bitch'! So I ups to him and I says, 'Ted, Tiny can't help that, came by it natural like 'cause he's a *dog*. But *you* had to work at it, sonny boy.' Should of heard what he said then."

Maggie boomed, "That Ted's just a bundle of nerves. Probably all that coffee they swill. Should stick to tea, or better yet, a pint of bitters. Nothing like a pint to calm the nerves."

Ackerson grinned. "And Maggie should know. Keeps her nerves calm with the bitters Harry smuggles in to her."

Hilary shook her bright head. "I suppose we shouldn't allow it," she told Miss Sanderson. "But what's the harm? Maggie enjoys her beer, so we turn a blind eye. Hey, here comes the other member of the Gang."

"Hail, hail, the gang's all here," Ackerson said morosely.

Harry was standing in the doorway and Hilary waved. He started toward them but Maggie was in full cry. "Harry, m'boy. Get right over here and give Maggie a kiss."

"How's my favorite girl?" he said as he dodged a woman on a walker and made his way to Maggie's side. He gave her not only a kiss but a hug and she beamed up at him. Then she pulled his head down and appeared to be whispering in his ear.

"Probably asking if he's made the weekly beer run," Ackerson said. "What in God's name is this pudding?"

"Bread and butter," Miss Sanderson told him.

"Ye gods!"

"You eat every scrap," Hilary told him. "We can't afford to hurt Mrs. Blecker's feelings. She works wonders with the food budget she gets. And another thing, Sean, no arguing with Harry."

He nodded and proceeded to spoon up his pudding. After tearing himself away from the former barmaid, Harry plumped himself down beside Miss Sanderson.

"We didn't expect to see you here today," Dorf said. "Aren't you going to have lunch?"

"Had a bite at the Fiddle. Nurse Daley rang up this morning when I was getting ready to drive over to Pendleton and asked me to deliver the meat order. So I had to drop everything and get it up here." Harry produced his cigar case and Ackerson raised his head and gave the other man a nasty smile. He silently pointed at the wall where a sign forbade smoking. "Hell!" Harry said, and turned to Miss Sanderson. "You enjoy the TV filming? Bet you never saw anything as heartwarming as those old folks and their dogs."

Miss Sanderson was spared from answering by the arrival of a tall, good-looking man in his early thirties. He carried a black leather bag and with his free hand tapped Harry's heavy shoulder. "Squeeze over there."

"Hello, Doc. Aren't you here on the wrong day?" Harry pulled his chair closer to Miss Sanderson's.

The doctor deposited his bag on the floor and sat down. "Regular examination day tomorrow but Nurse Daley called me about Nanny. Thought I'd better take a look at her."

"What's wrong—" Hilary broke off. "I'm forgetting my manners. Abigail, this is Ben Falkner. Ben, Abigail Sanderson."

Bending around the innkeeper's bulk, Falkner smiled at the secretary. "A pleasure, Miss Sanderson. I understand you're here to solve our trustees' dispute. With this bunch all I can say is good luck." His face sobered. "As for Nanny, Hilary, she's suffering from a terminal case of old age. Her heart's in bad shape and she hasn't much longer."

Hilary's full lips trembled and she bent her head. Dorf touched her hand and Ackerson put an arm around her shoulders. "Nanny's had a long and wonderful life," the antiques dealer murmured.

"I can't picture life without her," Hilary said sadly. "For as long as I can remember . . . and she seemed so well even a few months ago. She was still able to get around and she used to sit in the old nursery for hours. Then suddenly she was bedridden and just . . . just wasting away. Nanny's been waiting, you know, trying to live long enough to see Jamie again." Lifting her head, she looked appealingly at the doctor. "Ben, isn't there *anything* to be done? Treatment or medication? Should you call in a specialist?"

Falkner slowly shook his head. "Hilary, I'm afraid there's not one thing we can do. As I said she's very old, her heart is failing, and then there's this complication—"

"What complication?" Ackerson asked sharply.

The doctor looked from Hilary's distressed face to the antiques dealer. "Hasn't Nanny told you about—I suppose you'd call them bad dreams?"

Ackerson scowled. "She hasn't mentioned dreams, bad or otherwise, to me."

Falkner glanced from one trustee to another. Both Harry and Dorf looked puzzled, and Hilary said, "No, Nanny hasn't told any of us about dreams. Is she having nightmares?"

"Stop beating around the bush, Ben," Harry blurted. "Out with it."

"This is going to sound insane, but Nanny is convinced someone is entering her room at night, standing beside her bed, leaning over her—"

"Ye gods!" Ackerson threw his hands up. "It is *insane*. As though we haven't enough to contend with now and the old girl is going bonkers!"

"Shut up!" Twisting in his seat, Harry faced the doctor. "Could it be an aide? They check on Nanny at least once during the night."

"That's what I suggested to Nanny but she said no, said she'd know if it were an aide. I asked how and she told me she'd hear the rustle of a skirt, see the light from a flash. Nanny says this thing—"

"*Thing*," Miss Sanderson broke in. "Didn't she say whether it was a man or woman?"

"She doesn't know, Miss Sanderson. Said it's just a black figure. Claims something wakens her, she opens her eyes, and this thing is bending over her. All she can see is a dark form between her and the window."

"Bonkers!" Ackerson raged. "Absolutely gaga!"

"Hardly," Falkner told him coldly. "She's dreaming, of course, but to Nanny it's real, and not only is she terrified but it's putting more strain on her heart."

"How many times has she had this dream?" Miss Sanderson asked.

The doctor spread both hands. "Who knows? She said several times. Part of the problem is that she's alone so much. I tried to persuade her to let us move her down to a lower floor, where the other patients are, but you know how stubborn she can be. She really should have more visitors. Nanny loves to chat, and being alone day after day isn't good for her." Ackerson's mouth snapped open and Falkner said hastily, "I know how busy all of you are, and I know you're doing your best with this home and Nanny but—"

"Abigail," Hilary interrupted. "Are you planning to stay on here for a time? If you are, it would be kind if you would drop in and talk to Nanny for a time."

Miss Sanderson had planned to return to the inn for a much-needed rest, but the appeal in Hilary's eyes weakened that resolution. "I'd be happy to visit Nanny."

The doctor was leaning around Harry Moore again. He glanced at the remains of Miss Sanderson's lunch and then at her face. "If I were your physician I'd prescribe bed rest and aspirin."

"I've been taking that for over a week and it doesn't seem to work. But I am feeling somewhat better today."

Ackerson shoved his pudding bowl away. "Practicing medicine outside of office hours, Ben? Desperate for a new patient?"

Falkner smiled. "Speaking of office, better drop in and let me take that blood pressure again, Sean. Keep it up and either you're in stroke territory or you'll end up as cantankerous as old Josh Pitts."

"That's telling him, Doc," Harry said. "Say, while you're here, how about telling Abigail about the improvement in Josh and the other people since they got their dogs?"

"No, you don't!" The doctor jumped up and reached for his bag. "I'm staying neutral."

Harry's jaw jutted. "Maggie's a lot livelier now, isn't she?"

"She is. But whether that's Poopsie who did it or the beer you started smuggling in to her I can't say. Miss Sanderson, you have my sympathy. You're caught between an immovable object and an irresistible force." With that he hurried away.

"Some doctor," Harry muttered.

Ackerson jerked his bald head in agreement. "Impertinent young ass."

"Ben's a fine physician," Hilary defended. "He takes marvelous care of me."

"I've noticed that," Ackerman told her. "Doctor's pet patient."

Miss Sanderson glanced at the man. She could have sworn there was a note of bitter jealousy in his voice. Hilary ignored him, consulting her watch. "I've still some time left from my lunch break, Abigail. Would you like to have a look at the pavilion? We've managed to keep it as it was when Jamie lived there. It will give you an idea what the manor was once like."

At that point all Miss Sanderson wanted was to visit Nanny, return to the inn, curl up under the cozy duvet, and have a much-needed nap. But I'm sort of a guest, she reminded herself, and I'd better act like one. She agreed it would be a good idea and they went to retrieve their coats. As Hilary pulled her gloves on Miss Sanderson noticed one had been mended. She also noticed that although the other woman's coat and skirt were well cut and good material, they were showing signs of wear.

"We'll go out the rear door," Hilary said. "Down this hall. Oh, are you boys coming too? Harry, I thought you had to dash."

"A few minutes won't make that much difference. Kind of like to have a look at the pavilion. Been awhile."

Miss Sanderson glanced at the lines of closed doors. "This is a huge place."

Dorf nodded. "When I first came here as a child it was big enough to be scary. And there seemed an army of servants looking after it."

"Yes." Hilary's eyes were dreamy. "A housekeeper and cook and countless maids. How beautiful it was then!"

"As well as a squad of gardeners," Ackerson said gruffly. He opened the rear door. As they walked over uneven turf, he added, "These lawns were like velvet then, Abigail."

Miss Sanderson pulled her muffler closer to her throat. The sun had ducked behind a cloudbank and the breeze was chill. Hilary touched her arm and pointed. "That's where the rose garden used to be. Both Agnes and Aunt Marion loved roses, and at one time it was magnificent. That sundial was its center and the bushes were planted out from it like spokes in a wheel."

Looking at the sundial, Miss Sanderson said, "I didn't notice a rose garden in that group photo. I should have thought you'd have used it as a background."

"Most of the bushes had been killed by early frost the previous fall. Aunt Marion died that winter and with all the upset Agnes hadn't gotten around to having new bushes planted. The gardeners had dug over the beds and the raw earth looked unsightly." She pointed again. "The tennis court was over there and near it was a lovely grove of limes."

Harry stepped up beside Hilary. "I told Abigail the limes had to be taken down. Speaking of gardeners, where's Higgins?"

Ackerson scowled. "Probably in the kitchen with his feet up reading one of those trashy magazines of his. Higgins is bone lazy. I can never figure what he does here. He hasn't even bothered cutting the grass lately. I vote we get one of those gardening services who do a job."

"They wouldn't work for what we pay Higgins," Dorf told him.

"I know how we could raise some money if you'd—"

"Don't start that again, Sean," Hilary told him.

The antiques dealer turned his attention on Miss Sanderson. "The furniture in the pavilion is worth a mint. I've offered to sell it and not take a penny in commission. But Hilary won't listen, and Lee and Harry go along with her."

"And Hilary isn't listening now," that lady told him. "Here's the pavilion, Abigail. Behind this bank of hawthorns. Oh, dear, they do need trimming back. I must mention it to Higgins."

The pavilion was actually a small house. It was built of gray stone, and ivy softened the lines and crept along the mullioned windows that graced each side of the massive door. Opening her handbag, Hilary pulled out a ring of keys. The door opened into a wide hall that ran the length of the building. On the left-hand side were three doors, on the right only one. The hall was floored with parquet and mellow paneling covered walls.

Hilary opened the left-hand doors in turn. "Two bedrooms and a bath," she told the secretary. The bedrooms were charming, and Miss Sanderson could see what Ackerson had meant. The furnishings were antique and probably valuable. She found she was warm and loosened her muffler and unbuttoned her coat. "You keep heat on in here?"

"Of course," Hilary said.

"And cleaners come in weekly," Ackerson said. "No expense spared to cherish the shrine."

Crossing the hall, Hilary opened the door. This room, like the hall, ran the length of the building. At one end was a gleaming grand piano, Chippendale furniture dotted an Oriental rug, light streamed through silk curtains catching gleams from silver, copper, and bronze. An Adams fireplace dominated one wall and what looked like a Gobelin tapestry did the same on another. Despite its beauty the room had a lived-in look. Glancing around, Miss Sanderson saw why. Sheets of music were scattered over the piano top, a magazine was carelessly tossed on the seat of a wingback chair, a pair of leather slippers, one on its side, nestled on the hearth rug. In front of a window a rosewood desk bore a crystal decanter, a matching glass, an ashtray, and a gold pen.

Hilary, looking as much at home in the gracious room as its furnishings, beckoned from the far end of the room. On the piano top two silver-framed photographs perched among the sheet music. One was a head-and-shoulder shot of Hilary and Jamie. The young man's eyes looked dreamily into the viewer's. Neither was smiling but both looked happy. Miss Sanderson gazed from one young face to the other. Not only was their coloring similar but their features were almost identical. Broad brows, thin, high-bridged noses, tapering chins . . . She glanced at the woman beside her and again wondered how thirty years had made so little impact.

"Both Jamie and I took after the Coralunds," Hilary murmured. "We were third or fourth cousins and yet were continually mistaken for brother and sister. That's Jamie's father, Uncle Edmund, in the other picture. He was really a cousin too, but I always called him 'Uncle.' "

In the photograph Edmund Coralund looked in his sixties. He too had the fair beauty of his son and young cousin, but his bone structure was heavier, the face was coarser, his lips were fuller, and the lines were self-indulgent. Hilary was speaking again. "Uncle Edmund was the hell-raiser of that generation of Coralunds. I never knew his first wife, but heard she was a match for him. Poor little Aunt Marion didn't have a chance. I've often thought that's why she took to sprawling on lounges or staying in bed. Easier for her to be an invalid than to have to put up with her husband." She added, "But I never saw that side of Uncle Edmund. He always treated me as though I was made of porcelain."

Miss Sanderson touched a sheet of music. The paper was yellowed and brittle. Thirty years, she thought. "Jamie," Hilary told her proudly, "was a talented pianist. When all this happened he was living in London, studying for a musical career. Lee Dorf shared the flat with him. Lee, you were working on verse when—"

"Right," Dorf said. "I'd had one little book of verse published at that time. Jamie was planning on being a concert pianist and I was going to be a great poet. Later I tried novels but I failed miserably with those too."

"Right," Harry Moore agreed. "We all had big plans. I was going to be the best footballer in sports history." He rubbed a heavy thigh. "Shortly after Jamie took off I broke my hip, and that ended that dream."

Miss Sanderson looked at the fourth trustee. "And you, Sean?"

"Odd man out. The one with no talent. An uncle who had an antiques shop in Edinburgh took pity on me, and I was working as his apprentice. Nice old boy. Managed to imbue me with his enthusiasm and when he passed on made me his heir. I owe a lot to my uncle."

Including the Jaguar and expensive clothes, Miss Sanderson thought. She moved over to the desk. "Is this exactly the way it was when Jamie left?"

"As close to it as I can keep it," Hilary said. "I brought Jamie's tea down about eight in the morning. We'd had a silly quarrel the day before and I was going to try and make up with him." She gazed down at the desktop. "That ashtray was heaped with ashes and cigarette butts. Jamie smoked those foul black Russian cigarettes. The decanter was nearly empty and there was a little brandy in the glass. The letter he left for me was right here." Her finger touched a spot beside the gold pen. "I never let the cleaners touch his slippers or the magazines or music. I always come in and move them myself. The paper is brittle and could be damaged."

Miss Sanderson had a sudden image of those soft white hands carefully lifting those mementos, carefully replacing them in the exact position they had been in so many years before. Despite the warmth of the room she felt chilled. Harry must have felt the same because he shivered and said, "This is damn unhealthy, Hilary. Much as I hate siding with Sean, I agree it's time to call a halt. Let's sell these furnishings, use this place for something besides a—"

"Morgue," Ackerson chimed in. "Let the past die, darling. Let Jamie go."

Hilary Coralund didn't appear to hear either of them. She took a look at her watch and said brightly, "I must rush, Abigail. Flag day tomorrow."

Once outside the pavilion it was Harry who produced a ring of keys and locked the door. Miss Sanderson waited with him but the others circled the clump of hawthorn and Ackerson gave a howl. "Come and see what man's best friend is up to now!"

Trotting around the bushes, Miss Sanderson got a clear view of Tiny's sizable rump. The Great Dane was industriously excavating near the base of the sundial. He had an audience. Maggie's spaniel and the corgi were admiringly watching their mate's efforts.

Uttering an oath, Harry took off at a run. Even with his

strength there was a struggle before he pulled the big animal clear. "Someone get that ass Higgins," he shouted.

"The ass is here," a voice said. Higgins proved to be tall and scrawny and dour. "Whatta you want now?"

"You've got eyes, haven't you?" Harry raged. "Your job is to look after these grounds."

In one thin hand Higgins clutched a hoe. Leaning on it, he drawled, "Hired to be a gardener, not wrestle a dog that size. Better lock him up till he cools off. If you want you can use my tool shed."

"Excellent idea, Higgins," Ackerson snapped. "It's one place you seldom enter."

"If you ain't satisfied with my work, get someone else." Shouldering the hoe, Higgins lounged away.

"Higgins," Hilary called. "At least you can fill that hole in."

He paused and turned his head. "No use, miss. Filled that hole in more times than I can count. As soon as that dumb beast gets out he starts tearing and digging at it again."

Harry was tugging at the dog. "Tiny's dug other holes?"

"Does it all the time. Gotta admit he only does it in one place." Higgins gave a baying laugh. "Sure has a hankering to dig that chunk up. Must have buried a bone there. Stupid brute!"

"Higgins," Hilary said again. "It would be a great kindness if you would fill that hole in. It looks awful."

His eyes wandered over her lovely face and he softened a trifle. "Get to it as soon as time allows, miss."

"Which will be some time next year," Ackerson snarled. "What a day! Nanny has a thing in her room at night and that ruddy dog has a thing about destroying the grounds. I'm getting back to the shop. At least the only things there are antiques."

While the innkeeper, firmly grasping Tiny's collar,

pulled the big dog toward a wooden shed, Miss Sanderson scooped up the corgi and whistled to the spaniel. "Come along, Poopsie, time to get back to Maggie."

"You're very good," Hilary said gratefully. "You will remember Nanny, won't you?"

"I'll not forget," Miss Sanderson said.

As she walked toward the house she checked to see that Poopsie was at her heels and held the corgi well out in front of her. I'll take no chance, she thought, of Cleo tinkling all over my coat.

"I don't doubt that. But Tiny's punishment is just to be locked up until he cools down. He was tearing up the lawn."

"Dogs will be dogs." Maggie took a closer look at Miss Sanderson. "Got a nasty cold, have you, dearie? Tell you what I always use. Stout. Clears the nostrils right up."

Miss Sanderson confessed, "I've been relying on whiskey and brandy."

"Never cared for spirits but always like my pint."

Miss Allingham decided to contribute her remedy for colds. "I don't hold with alcohol in *any* form. Chamomile tea and honey and lemon do a much better job."

Noticing the sour expression on Miss Allingham's gaunt face, Miss Sanderson could believe the lemon part. She turned her attention to Maggie. "Could you tell me where Nanny Balfour has her room? This floor or—"

"Bless me, no. Way up on the third floor. Still in the room she had when the Coralund family lived here. Right next to the old nursery. Nanny's the only patient on that floor. She—"

"Rank favoritism!" Miss Allingham announced. She pushed steel-rimmed glasses up on a sharp nose. "Gets the best of food too. Kept well away from the rest of us poor people. Too good for us!"

Maggie was more charitable. "Don't talk nonsense. Nanny's always been part of the Coralund family. Remember well when I was working at the Fiddle. I heard Mr. Jamie even gave Nanny presents on Mother's Day. He was that fond of her. And Nanny's the oldest person in this house."

"She is *not*. I know for a fact that Mrs. Rome is two months older—"

"You got that wrong. Two months *younger*."

Giving up that argument, Miss Allingham turned her venom on Miss Sanderson. "As for you, can't see where you've any call to see Nanny Balfour. You're nothing but a stranger to her."

CHAPTER 5

Catching sight of Rose's dumpling form hastening down the hall, Miss Sanderson called a question. "In the lounge, miss. Maggie and Miss Allingham. Josh, thank goodness, is napping." In a whirl of blue and white the aide ducked into a doorway.

The dog owners were in the lounge with a half-dozen other patients. Their brief fling with starry fame seemed to have run its course, and all eyes were locked on the television screen. A cooking show was in progress. Miss Sanderson stood for a moment watching an elaborate dessert being prepared. Then she dumped Cleo in Miss Allingham's lap. Poopsie was already having an emotional reunion with his mistress, and Maggie, cooing endearments, hugged him to her bosom. Miss Allingham seemed less than pleased and offered no thanks to Cleo's rescuer. The former barmaid more than made up for her dour companion.

"Awful good of you, dearie. Those aides just took Poopsie and Cleo and Tiny and shoved them outside. Where Tiny?"

"Being punished."

"Better not beat him. Josh will be riled and he can fierce."

"Nobody's a stranger long to Nanny," Maggie said warmly.

Miss Sanderson had had enough of Miss Allingham. She turned to Maggie. "You say Nanny's on the third floor?"

"Take the lift, dearie. My Harry had it installed a number of years ago and it sure helps."

Miss Allingham entered the fray. "You talk about Harry Moore as though he *owns* this place. Actually, it was the board of trustees who installed that lift. Your Harry was the one who stuck us with these disgusting animals." To emphasize her point, she shoved Cleo off her lap.

Maggie seemed struck dumb, and it was Miss Sanderson who rebutted. "If you didn't want a dog, why did you take one?"

"Because they were handing them out free and I take anything I can get free. Any time they want they can have that little devil back. As for you, young lady, don't you dare go haring off to Nanny on your own. Nurse Daley runs this place. Get her permission."

Miss Sanderson rather liked the "young lady" bit. No one had called her that for more years than she could remember. She didn't care for the rest of Miss Allingham's statement. Lifting her chin, she said haughtily, "I don't need the nurse's permission. I have Dr. Falkner's." Spinning on her heels, she left the lounge while she was winning.

Age, she thought wrathfully. It doesn't make one wise or mellow or kind. All the years seem to do is make one even more bitter, like Miss Allingham, or even nicer, like Maggie Murphy. As she located the lift she wondered what the years had done to Nanny Balfour.

The lift, large enough to handle a stretcher, rose smartly to the third floor. A long vista of hall opened in front of her. Doors lined it and monotonous gray covered everything in sight. She tried several doors and found

nothing behind them but trunk rooms and storage areas.
Toward the end of the hall she was rewarded for her
efforts. This door opened onto a nursery. She stepped
into the room and time reeled backward to her own nursery, and to the one in the Forsythe manor in Sussex
where Robby's electric train and toy soldiers had once
entertained a small boy.

In this nursery the walls were papered in ivory with
faded pink-and-blue rocking horses rocking around the
ceiling border. Tiers of white-painted shelves held ranks
of dolls and stuffed animals and children's books. Against
oak flooring the tracks of a boy's train coiled in a figure
eight. There were two tiny rocking chairs and one large
one. On one perched a plush teddy bear, the other held
a Raggedy Ann, black button eyes glinting in the light from
the window. On the seat of the large rocking chair was a
cushion displaying a garland of petit-point flowers.

Abigail picked up a book. From its cover Christopher
Robin and his friend Pooh looked out. She turned a page
and from careful childish printing she learned that this
book had once belonged to James Hareford Coralund. A
book of nursery rhymes had once been Edmund Coralund's, and Hilary Coralund had been the owner of the
Three Little Pigs. Carefully she replaced the books. Edmund
was dead, his son had vanished, Hilary was living a ghost
life, and these fragile books still survived.

Giving herself a mental shake, she returned to the present and Nanny Balfour. At the far end of the nursery were
two doors. One opened into a bathroom, the other—ah,
this was where the old nurse lived. She stepped into the
room and looked at the high bed. The woman in it was so
tiny she hardly made a mound under the spread. In a face
like a shrunken apple, the eyes were closed. A snowy wisp
of hair curled from under a pink bedcap and hands like
claws lay on the spread. Nanny seemed to be having a nap.

Miss Sanderson glanced around the room. It was charming. Here there was no gray paint or linoleum. Nanny must like flowers because the wallpaper was dotted with blooms, roses rambled on the curtains, cushions on the two chairs sported more floral petit point, and a vase of fresh roses wafted fragrance from the bed table.

She was about to tiptoe out of the room when a voice stopped her. "Nurse?" The nightcap rolled on the pillow and bright eyes swept over Miss Sanderson. "Not a nurse. Are you a new volunteer come to read to me?"

"No, I'm—" Miss Sanderson stopped. What exactly was she? A stranger here to meddle in the home's business was about the aptest description. "I'm acquainted with Hilary Coralund and the other trustees. Hilary suggested you might like me to visit you for a few moments."

"Ah, the children. So busy, poor dears. So thoughtful too. So good of you to take time for an old lady. Do take this chair near the bed. It seems difficult now to even turn my head. Perhaps you'd care for a little sherry? You'll find it in the top drawer of the bureau. No, none for me. I used to enjoy a drop of sherry but . . . What is your name, my dear?" Miss Sanderson poured sherry and told Nanny her name. "I shall call you Abigail. You seem so young to me. But then anyone under sixty is beginning to seem like a child. The children are around your age and I still think of them as tots. That photo on the bureau, the one in the wooden frame, that's my children when they were . . . well, Jamie was eight so the other boys were eight too. Hilary was eighteen months younger than Jamie."

The top of the bureau was crowded with photographs and knickknacks but Miss Sanderson had already noticed the picture Nanny mentioned. In it a group of boys clustered around a little girl. Hilary wore a ruffled party dress and a satin ribbon threaded through glossy curls. She had no trouble picking out Jamie and Harry, who even at eight had been a husky lad, but she couldn't decide which small blond boy was Sean and which was Lee Dorf. She asked the old nurse. "Which one is Lee?"

"The boy on Jamie's left. That picture was taken before his nose was broken. His father did that. A terrible man Amos Dorf was, cruel to his poor wife, and after her death he turned his ill temper on Lee. A drunkard and a beast. It's a pity he didn't die sooner."

Harsh judgment, Miss Sanderson thought, and took the chair beside the bed. She sneezed and reached hastily for a handkerchief. Nanny's bright eyes blinked. "A spring cold is the worse kind. They linger. I always used mustard plasters for chest colds and raw garlic for head colds. You mince the garlic up fine and sprinkle a little salt on it. I promise that has a head cold on the run in no time."

As well as anyone else in the immediate vicinity, Miss Sanderson decided, and wondered how Aggie had missed this one in her long list of remedies. She realized that now she was there she had no idea what to chat about. It might not be a good idea to discuss Jamie Coralund, that might distress his old nurse. She thought of Project Giftdog and discarded it also. Finally she said, "I passed through the nursery and it took me back years, in fact, back to my own childhood. I couldn't resist looking at the books. Did you take care of Edmund Coralund when he was a child?"

Nanny chuckled. "Hardly, my dear. I came to work here when Jamie was three weeks old and Mr. Edmund was in his fifties. I was in my early forties. Jamie was a late child for Mr. Edmund, you see. He had a daughter who was twenty-five when Jamie was born. Agnes's mother was Mr. Edmund's first wife."

"Hilary mentioned that her uncle—"

"Second cousin. But Hilary always called him uncle. I've no doubt she told you what a hell-raiser Mr. Edmund was. Born out of his time I've always thought. Mr. Edmund used to boast his three interests in life were wenching, horses, and drinking. In that order. And he proved it. Sowed his wild oats right up to the time he had his first stroke. His second wife, Miss Marion, couldn't start to handle him. She was a timid mousy woman and he nearly drove her wild." Nanny chuckled again and winked an eye. "When he sent for Hilary and I saw how much the child looked like Jamie, I couldn't help but wonder if she was another of Mr. Edmund's wood colts. That's the term he always used. Mr. Edmund always joked a lot with me, and when I mentioned that he just roared with laughter. Told me it was impossible because Hilary's mother was an Australian and had never set foot out of that country and he'd never stirred out of England. Great man for a joke was Mr. Edmund. Kind to children too. Treated Hilary like his own daughter and did everything he could for the three boys. He liked young ones around and encouraged Harry, Sean, and Lee to visit Jamie. Swear for years those three were here more than at their own homes."

Nanny had run out of breath. She wheezed and one veined hand toyed with the edge of the coverlet. Her flannel nightgown matched the pink nightcap, and the wizened lips were well dabbed with pale-pink lip rouge. Even at nearly the century mark some female vanity must linger. The pink lips opened in a tiny yawn and Miss Sanderson said quickly, "I mustn't tire you."

"My dear, I'm always tired. For the last few months I seem to drift in and out, nod off even in the middle of a sentence. Joanne Parker came up to read to me yesterday and I slept most of the time she was here." A finger pointed at the bed table. Beside the vase of roses was a novel with a bright dust jacket. "Lee brings up library books he thinks might interest me but they're usually dull as dishwater. That one certainly is. But if I do nod off please don't go. It gets lonely up here with nothing but memories for company."

"Perhaps you should have them move you down with the other patients. To give you some company."

"Sean suggested that but I said no. This has been my room for over half a century. I see you're looking at my pillow slip. Pretty, isn't it?"

It was pretty. The white linen was edged with a wide border of what looked like handmade lace. "Did you tat the lace, Nanny?"

"Indeed I did. I've always been a great hand for needle-work. I made this lace for Miss Marion's pillows shortly after I came here. Course the slips wore out twice, but I took off the lace and put it on new ones. The last time I wasn't able to handle it and Hilary did it for me. The children are so kind to me. Hilary sends flowers and Harry brings me sherry and . . ." Eyelids, like old parchment, drifted down. Miss Sanderson was alarmed and bent forward but Nanny was breathing evenly. In the midst of a sentence she had drifted into sleep. Miss Sanderson considered leaving and then sat back. This beflowered room was peaceful and heartwarming. It seemed far from a hectic world, far from disturbances in the Persian Gulf, fear of a stock market crash, rumors of impending war and terrorism. Then she jumped. Nanny was talking again, her voice a mere whisper, her eyes still closed.

"It's no use arguing, darling, this is the only way. You know how your dear mother and father counted on this. Agnes too . . . No, I don't agree . . . Jamie, you must have a home and children . . . no, the other one can never give you those . . . I don't care what you say . . . if your father knew he'd be rolling in the grave . . . don't take on, darling, Nanny knows best."

Talking in her sleep, Miss Sanderson thought, and moved uncomfortably. She felt like an eavesdropper. Then the eyelids fluttered and Nanny said, "I forget what I was saying, my dear."

"You were telling me about the children, how kind they are to you."

"So I was. Sean offered to get me a television set but I told him I'd rather look at the ceiling. They come to visit often too. Lee was here last night, no, it must have been two nights ago. I tell them all not to worry so much about me. They have their own lives and running this place takes so much time. But they never forget Nanny Balfour. And Nanny loves all—" A soft tap sounded at the hall door and she broke off. The door opened and Nanny said, "Is it dinnertime already, Rose? From the smell of chicken I guess we're having a treat."

The dumpling aide bustled in carrying a tray. The heavy white china used in the dining room wasn't used for Nanny Balfour. Her tray was set with dainty bone china covered with tiny sprays of pink roses. The aide set the tray on a side table and opened the door of a closet. She reached down a plump pillow. "Now, to make you comfy, Nanny."

"Let me help." Miss Sanderson jumped up and lifted Nanny's frail shoulders while Rose positioned the pillow. Miss Sanderson caressed the border of fragile lace.

"Now, don't forget to take that pillow out again, Rose. I don't care to be propped up like this."

"I never forget, Nanny." Rose snapped down the short legs on the bed tray. "I'll cut up the chicken for you."

"Child, I can still handle a fork and knife. Abigail, you're leaving now? I've so enjoyed our little chat. If you have time would you drop in again?"

Miss Sanderson smiled down at her. "I think I may be leaving town tomorrow but I will certainly come in and say good-bye to you. It's been a pleasure meeting you, Nanny."

When Miss Sanderson stepped out of the lift she saw

Nurse Daley, a sheaf of forms in one hand, bent over the desk. She raised her head. "Ah, Miss Sanderson. Miss Allingham tells me you went up to visit Nanny Balfour. Nice of you. She's a darling and we all love her. Have you . . . ah, have you come to a decision yet?"

"Not as yet," Miss Sanderson told her, and made her way to the carpark. As she drove back to the inn she knew she had been evasive with the nurse. Her decision, and it had proved difficult, had been made while she sat quietly in Nanny Balfour's flowery room.

She decided it only fair to tell Harry Moore first.

CHAPTER 6

When Miss Sanderson reached the Fiddle and Bow she found a message waiting from Hilary Coralund. Using the public phone booth, she rang Hilary's number. Their conversation was brief, seemingly much too brief for Hilary, but Miss Sanderson firmly stopped the flow of words, mentioned they'd soon all know, and went in search of Harry Moore. Although the bar was doing a good business there was no sign of the inn's genial proprietor. Mrs. Moore was working the taps and passing out pints while a sullen-faced girl handed out meat pies and salad. Miss Sanderson asked, "Has Harry got back from Pendleton yet?"

"Came back about an hour ago," Mrs. Moore told her. "Just in time to get another call from that Coralund woman. But this time she wanted you. Did you get her message?"

"I did, thank you. Where can I find Harry?"

"In his office. He's dead beat again." Mrs. Moore shoved a couple of steins across the counter. "Got enough to do right here and then having to run his legs off after that home. Doesn't seem right. Harry's getting no younger." She glanced up. "Will you be wanting supper?"

Miss Sanderson had been eyeing the meat pies dubiously. "I'll get something later."

Harry's office proved to be more of a den than a place of business. There was a desk, piled high with account books, but the room was crowded with bookcases, a massive chest of drawers, and two rump-sprung chairs before a roaring fire. The air was blue with cigar smoke and smelled richly of brandy fumes. Harry was sprawled comfortably by the hearth, a cigar in one hand, a squat glass in the other. Miss Sanderson regarded him approvingly. A man after my own heart, she thought. He made a move to get up but she waved him back. "Sit. Your wife tells me you're worn out."

"That I am. What a lousy day this has been. How are you feeling?"

"Much better. Country air seems to agree with me."

"Too bad it doesn't perk up your appetite. My wife says you've hardly eaten a bite. Seeing you're so perky, Abigail, you can pour your own drink. Dribble a bit in my glass too, please."

She complied and sank down opposite, stretching long, shapely legs out to the fire. She glanced up at the line of photographs on the mantel and her host told her, "My mom and dad. I took after Mom in looks. She was tall and dark and husky too. That next one is Sally and me in our wedding picture. She was a comely lass then. Those are our sons, taken when they were in their teens. The older boy favors his mother but Harry Junior is the spitting image of his pop. Both boys are married now, and Alan has a kid of his own." He sighed. "Time marches on."

Not only was the younger boy the image of his father, but Sally Moore had indeed been a comely lass. Miss Sanderson found it hard to believe that the woman with the bitter mouth she had just left in the bar was the round-faced girl with the radiant smile in the wedding picture. Perhaps the reason for the change was not only the years but the lovely woman in the next photograph.

From this one Hilary smiled, and Miss Sanderson decided it must have been taken recently. The hairstyle was the one Hilary was currently wearing. At the far end of the mantel was the group photograph she had seen at the Guild Hall.

Harry must have been following her eyes because he said, "Agnes gave all of us a copy of that. So we wouldn't forget Jamie, she said. Small chance of that!" His eyes flickered and fastened on his companion's face. "What did Hilary want? Never mind. Pushing you for an answer, I'll bet."

"You win the bet." Miss Sanderson drained her glass and rose to refill it. "We're meeting at eleven tomorrow morning at the Guild Hall and—"

"And you'll side with Hilary and Lee and Sean."

"Not exactly, Harry. I'm going to tell you my decision now. If you don't want to attend the meeting you won't have—"

"What *exactly* is 'not exactly'? That's like saying a girl's a little bit pregnant. Either you're with them or not with them."

"There's such a thing as compromise."

He didn't appear to be listening. His eyes were fixed on the leaping flames. "Right from the start I knew it was a hare-brained scheme. But going up to the home all the time ... seeing those poor old devils having to give up everything that made their lives worthwhile ..."

"Nanny Balfour certainly doesn't lack for personal possessions."

"She's the only one who has them. Rest of the patients ... oh, they have albums, little knickknacks, but that's all. I figured if they had a dog, something to pet and love—Hell! Now I'll have to tell Maggie and old Josh to say goodbye to their dogs!"

"Harry Moore! Will you *listen* to me?" She had his attention and gave him a reassuring smile. "I could see almost immediately that Mr. Perkins's plan was not realistic. If it goes into being Nurse Daley will resign, and I have no doubt the rest of the staff will follow her example. If there were funds to care for a number of dogs and provide proper kennels it could work. But there aren't and—"

"You're sure cheering me up, Abigail."

"If you don't shut up I'm going to brain you. I'm going to tell the other trustees that Project Giftdog is canceled but that the dogs already in the home are staying there."

The big man lunged to his feet. His glass slid and brandy spattered on the hearth. Paying no attention to this, he grabbed both her shoulders. "You mean I won't have to tell Josh and Maggie? They can keep their dogs and—"

"That's what I meant by compromise. Harry, turn loose. You're bruising my shoulders."

"Sorry. Abigail, this calls for a celebration." He picked up his glass and took the one she was extending. "This is one heavy weight off my shoulders."

She was gingerly rubbing her own shoulder. She was glad she hadn't told him she was approving the entire project. He'd probably have crippled her. Returning to his chair, he gave her a wide smile. Then the smile faltered. "You can't do it. Soon as that dog food company hears about it they'll pick up the dogs and—"

"They can have two of them. Miss Allingham detests her corgi and I doubt the other woman wants her dog."

"Mrs. Safrin is so confused she doesn't *know* she has a dog. But how will you do it?"

Miss Sanderson had been lighting a cigarette. As the smoke mingled with cigar fumes, she told him, "Mr. William Perkins sounds like a nice gentleman. I can't see him ripping away Tiny and Poopsie from elderly people who love them. If necessary, I'll make a personal appeal to him."

Harry stroked his jutting chin. "Can't see them continuing to send dog food. And what about vet expenses and—"

"Not to worry. Let me handle that. Perhaps I can raise funds to cover expenses, including a boy to exercise the dogs."

"Not in this town, you won't." He flipped his cigar end into the fire. "We've about drained it dry."

She gave him her gamine grin. "I have a germ of an idea on how to raise the money. Now, any other questions?"

He lighted another cigar, sipped brandy, crossed his legs and then uncrossed them, and finally said, "Not a question but I do have a kind of favor to ask."

"Ask away."

"Maggie. And old Josh too. They've been pretty upset lately. Rumors flying about taking away their dogs and all that sort of thing. Would you mind reassuring them? Tell them yourself they needn't fret. If I do it they'll figure Maggie's boy is just offering them a sugar tit. And Maggie's a grand girl. The Fiddle's never seen another barmaid to compare with Maggie Murphy. Since she left most of them are like that sulky girl we got now. Maggie! How she brightened that bar up! Remember when I was a kid hearing howls of laughter when she was behind the bar. My dad used to say Maggie was better than any floor show. We won't see her like again."

Miss Sanderson mulled his request over. "Directly after the trustee meeting in the morning I was planning on driving back to London. But I understand what you mean, Harry. Tell you what, I'll get up early and drop into the home before the meeting. I'll assure Maggie and Josh they needn't worry, the dogs are theirs."

Leaning forward, he patted her knee, and this time the huge hand was gentle. "And you're a grand lady too, Abigail Sanderson. Funny, we only met a couple of days ago and I feel we've been friends for years."

"I feel the same way, Harry." Also, Miss Sanderson silently admitted, I admire this ex-footballer turned innkeeper who cherishes dogs and feels deeply for the old and lonely. She sat dreamily, lulled by the peace of the room, the crackle of the fire.

Harry's deep voice broke through that dream. "Care for a slice of fruitcake, Abigail? Goes good with brandy."

She nodded and he sliced a rich moist cake and looked in vain for a plate or a napkin. They settled for paper tissues. Miss Sanderson demolished her slice in record time. "Did your wife bake this? It's delicious."

"My sister-in-law. Sally doesn't have much time for baking. The kitchen and bar work run her ragged." He crumpled his tissue and tossed it into the flames. "Sometimes I wonder what life would have been like if Jamie had stayed. He and Hilary would have been married and the rest of us . . . maybe Sean and Lee would have found girls and got married. Lee might not be so distant and kind of cold, and Sean might not have a disposition like a bear with a sore paw."

"You were lucky to have found Sally."

"Sally wasn't so lucky, poor lass. She's been a good wife, gave me two fine sons, works her fingers to the bone, frets about me. And me . . . Hilary crooks her little finger and I go running. Would you believe the night our second son was born I wasn't even at the hospital? The furnace at the home went on the blink and Hilary called for me. I left my wife in childbirth and went up to fix it."

Miss Sanderson's lips firmed. "If a person doesn't care for a situation, he changes it."

"Good in theory but sometimes theories don't work in practice. Maybe Lee and Sean and I are weak. Maybe we're trying to take the place of the husband Hilary never had. I don't know what it is but I do know the four of us are bound by something we seem powerless to break."

Harry had said he wasn't good with words, but the words

he'd just said conjured up rather a horrible picture of three men and a beautiful woman tied together with invisible but strong chains. The innkeeper continued talking in a low voice, but Miss Sanderson leaned back her head and closed her eyes. The combination of warmth and brandy was making her drowsy. The next thing she knew a hand was gently shaking her. "Abigail, best be off to bed. You went to sleep."

She blinked and yawned. The flames had burned down to glowing coals. She glanced at her watch. Not even eight and she was exhausted. "I'm as bad as Nanny Balfour. Did I chatter in my sleep like she does?"

He laughed. "You snored a couple of times but didn't say a word. I know what you mean about Nanny. When I dropped in last week she dozed most of the time I was there. Kept rambling on about me being a naughty boy and not wiping the mud off my shoes. Funny thing was I could remember when Nanny gave me hell for that. I was only about seven."

Stifling another yawn, Miss Sanderson rose. She decided to skip supper and go directly to bed. Harry looked up at her. "You won't forget about Maggie and Josh?"

She patted his arm. "I'll be at the home bright and early. I'll set my alarm."

When her alarm sounded at a quarter to seven the following morning, she buried her face in a pillow, vainly willing for it to stop. It didn't and she rolled over and punched it off. As she pulled herself out from under the cosy duvet she decided she might be early but was far from bright. Coffee might have helped but she didn't bother stopping for it. She decided she'd reassure the dog owners, go to the trustee meeting, and then head back to London. As a reward, along the way she'd stop and have a decent meal.

Another reward was the sun glancing off the hood of the MG. The sky was clear, and it looked as though it was going to be a fine day. The fineness of that day lasted until she stepped into the foyer of the home. As usual the desk was deserted, but on a straight chair near it a forlorn figure huddled. Maggie Murphy had a shawl bundled around her plump shoulders and her flaming head drooped over the spaniel clutched in her arms.

Miss Sanderson went directly to the older woman and Maggie lifted swollen wet eyes. "So, you come to kill Poopsie too." She thrust the dog out. "Here, take him but please, miss, don't kill him like you did Tiny."

"What on earth are you talking about?"

"First Tiny, now Josh, and . . ." Maggie proceeded to weep in earnest.

Miss Sanderson searched in her bag and found a clean handkerchief. She handed it to Maggie and put the dog back in the old woman's lap. "Get a grip on yourself. I came here because Harry Moore asked me to tell both Josh and you that you're going to keep your pets. I give you my word no one is going to take them away from you."

Maggie's eyes searched the other woman's face and then she gulped and swabbed at her cheeks. "You got an honest face, dearie, and I believe you but, if you didn't poison Tiny, who did?"

Poison? Miss Sanderson thought and pulled up another chair and sat down. She put a comforting arm around the trembling shoulders of Maggie Murphy. "Start from the beginning and tell me about Tiny."

"It was last evening. Josh was all het up because you locked his dog up. He wouldn't touch a bite of his supper and kept yelling and cussing till Nurse Evans—she's the night nurse, dearie—sent the night orderly, young Tom, out about nine to get Josh's dog. Tom come back and told Nurse Evans the dog was dead, foam all around his muzzle, poisoned. Josh heard and he had some kind of attack. Fell right down. Nurse figured it was his heart or maybe a stroke and she rang up Dr. Falkner—"

"God," Miss Sanderson breathed. "Is Josh . . ."

To her relief the red curls shook. "He was took bad but the doctor he give Josh a shot and they carried him up to the sickroom. The doctor was with him most of the night, and I didn't get a wink of sleep."

"Is Josh going to be all right?"

"He's still pretty sick but the doctor says he'll live. Tough man, Josh Pitts. If he finds out who did for Tiny he'll go for the cowardly beast." Maggie Murphy blew her nose. "Doctor just nicely left and then the day shift come on. Rose took up Nanny's tea like she always does and then Rose she came storming down and say's Nanny's dead. Nurse Daley was coming in when Rose comes down, and she phones the doctor again. The three of them are up with Nanny now." Maggie broke down again. "It's more than a body can stand!"

"Dear God! Nanny!" Miss Sanderson said brokenly.

She lifted the old woman from her chair and put an arm around her waist. "Have you had breakfast?"

"Dining room don't open for twenty minutes yet, dearie."

"I'll settle you in the lounge and you stay there until breakfast is served. Then you're going to bed and get some rest."

As she helped the woman into a comfortable chair, Maggie looked tearfully up at her. "They won't let dogs in the dining room and I'm not stirring a step without my Poopsie."

"Take Poopsie with you. If anyone objects you tell them you have my permission and that dog stays with you or they'll have me to deal with."

"I'll tell them, dearie. Where are you going?"

"To Nanny Balfour's room." As Miss Sanderson reached the lift she caught sight of blue-and-white stripes. "Come here, Flossie. You take a cup of tea into Maggie Murphy in the lounge. Right now!"

The girl's eyes widened at Miss Sanderson's tone. "Yes, miss."

"And be sure to tell whoever is in charge of the dining room that Maggie has my permission to take her dog in with her."

"But the rules are—"

"To *hell* with the rules. That woman is not only exhausted but terrified. Keep this up and she's going to be sick. As soon as Maggie has breakfast you take her to her room. Get her into bed and that dog stays right with her." Miss Sanderson drew herself up. "I represent Miss Agnes Coralund and what I say around here goes. Understand?"

The aide nodded her understanding and backed away from the icy rage in the older woman's face. When she reached the third floor Miss Sanderson found the door to the nursery open. She circled the train set and rapped at the door of the beflowered room. Without waiting for a response, she swung it open.

Nurse Daley and the doctor were bending over the bed and Rose huddled in a far corner. Her plump face was wet with tears. Both the nurse and the doctor glanced up. Ben Falkner's good-looking face was drawn with fatigue. "If you came to see Nanny," he said, "you're too late. She died in the night. Probably in her sleep."

"A peaceful way to go," the nurse murmured.

"I found her," Rose shakily volunteered. "This morning when I brought her tea."

Nanny Balfour looked much as she had the previous day when Miss Sanderson had watched her as she dozed. The doctor straightened and pressed a hand against the small of his back. "I've been expecting her to slip away, but it's going to be hard breaking it to Hilary."

"Miss Coralund was here shortly before I went off duty

yesterday," Nurse Daley said. "She was coming up to spend a little while with Nanny. All the trustees were so fond of Nanny. The staff was fond of her too."

"I'll miss her," Rose blurted. "Always so nice spoken. Not like some of the patients, whining and complaining like they do."

Miss Sanderson was standing in front of the bureau. She picked up the picture of Nanny's children. "Did any of the other trustees visit her last evening?"

The nurse said crisply, "The only one I saw was Miss Coralund. Of course, they could have come later, I go off duty at six and we didn't insist on visiting hours for Nanny."

Miss Sanderson moved restlessly to the window and gazed down. She could see the mass of unkempt hawthorn bushes and she spotted the slate roof and chimney pots of Jamie's retreat. Off to the right was the sundial. Suddenly she bent forward and stared down. Her hand moved to her face and a thumbnail started clicking against her front tooth. In the quiet room it resounded.

"Miss Sanderson," the nurse called, "*what* are you doing?"

"Thinking." And tapping my tooth—a bad habit, Miss Sanderson added silently, and one Robby complains about. Turning back to the room, she gazed around. Then she bent, felt under the bed, and pulled out an object. She held it up. "Nurse Daley, are your aides in the habit of throwing pillows on the floor?"

"Of course not! The extra pillow is kept in that closet on the shelf. Nanny prized those lace-trimmed slips. Now how—"

"Nanny could have pushed it off the bed," the doctor said impatiently.

"No!" Rose took a step forward. "I don't think so, Doctor. You see, the only times Nanny had that extra pillow under her head was when she had meals or tea. She couldn't abide it there all the time. Said it made her neck stiff. All the aides were careful to remove that extra pillow and put it back on the shelf."

"Which aide was on duty here last night?" Miss Sanderson asked.

Nurse Daley frowned. "Probably Mollie Carlyle. But I'd have to check Nurse Evans's records to be certain."

"But you do know the movements of the night staff. With Nanny Balfour, I mean."

"Of course. Occasionally Nurse Evans and I switch shifts. Compared with day shift, night shift is calm and peaceful. Let me see . . ."

Rose tried to assist. "I helped Nanny with her dinner and then gave her a bit of a wash before I went off duty, nurse. As I was getting out of the lift in the foyer, Miss Coralund stepped onto it. She asked how Nanny was and I said fine. Then—"

"Very good, Rose." Nurse Daley cut off the flood of words. "An aide would check in on Nanny about seven and then at half-past eight she'd prepare the patient for the night. Give Nanny a back rub and her medication. After that if Nanny needed anything she could push this buzzer. The final check would be about one in the morning. Just to look in on the patient." She straightened her cap. "Why all the questions, Miss Sanderson? Do you feel Nanny's death was due to our negligence?"

Miss Sanderson's cool blue eyes sought the doctor. "Will there be a postmortem?"

"No, it won't be necessary. As I mentioned to you yesterday, Nanny's heart was in bad shape and I was expecting her to pass on at any time." His voice sharpened. "I think you owe us an explanation. Why the inquisition?"

The secretary didn't answer in words. Instead she held up the plump pillow and pointed. The doctor frowned, and both he and the nurse stepped closer. "All I see is a tiny stain so faint I can hardly make it out."

"A pink smear," Miss Sanderson said flatly.

"Nanny's lip rouge," the nurse said, and smiled. "She insisted on wearing it, even at night. I remember her telling me once that no matter the age a woman was always a *woman*. Look, you can still see the remains of some of it in the wrinkles on her lips."

Miss Sanderson willed her eyes away from the waxen face on the lace-trimmed pillow. "How do you explain a smear of lip rouge on this pillow?"

"Any number of ways." Nurse Daley shrugged a white nylon shoulder. "When the aide turned her on her side for the alcohol rub. Perhaps in her sleep Nanny rolled her face around."

"On a pillow that wasn't in use? Observe the location of this stain. In the center of the pillow slip. I have a hunch if this stain was magnified you might see the full imprint of Nanny's lips."

After taking the pillow from the secretary's hands, Dr. Falkner held it up. "She could be right. Nurse, what do you think?"

The nurse swung on Miss Sanderson. "Are you implying—"

"I'm suggesting that pillow might have been pressed down on Nanny's face. And I'm strongly urging that you listen to me."

"And I am strongly suggesting you have a wild imagination." The nurse's eyes met the doctor's. "But better safe than sorry. Perhaps . . ."

He placed the pillow carefully at the foot of the bed. "I shan't sign the death certificate until this is checked out. I'll ring up Inspector Taylor and until he arrives we'll keep this room locked. Does that satisfy you, Miss Sanderson?"

It did. As they stepped out of the lift and into the foyer, she asked, "Do you know where I can find Higgins?"

Nurse Daley was hurrying toward her office but she

called back, "Mrs. Blecker will know. She'll be in the dining room."

Mrs. Blecker was in the dining room, majestically pre-
siding behind the counter. Most of the patients were lined
up in front of it and only three sat at tables. Two women
with walkers waited for their breakfasts at one table and
at another Maggie Murphy sat, clutching her dog and
staring defiantly around. Flossie was carrying a tray of
food to Maggie. Heading directly to the counter, Miss
Sanderson pushed in between a couple of patients. One
was Miss Allingham and she was complaining to the cook.
"I do think, Mrs. Blecker, you might occasionally give us
bacon and eggs. We haven't had them for a long time."

"We had bacon and eggs last Thursday." Mrs. Blecker
continued placidly spooning up steaming porridge.

"Well, we haven't had sausage or—" Breaking off, Miss
Allingham snarled, "Stop pushing and shoving and get to
the end of the line! Oh, it's *you*! Miss Sanderson, I do think
it's mighty high-handed letting Maggie bring that filthy
animal in here. We do have rules, you know!"

Miss Sanderson resisted a strong impulse to tell her what
to do with the rules. Restraining herself, she called over
Miss Allingham's bobbing head, "Mrs. Blecker, could you
tell me where I can find Higgins?"

"He was in earlier for breakfast. My daughter might
know. Lift that panel at the end of the counter and come
in." She jerked her head. "Carol's back there."

"Back there" proved to be a long, narrow room that
might once have been a butler's pantry. A plump girl who
bore a striking resemblance to the cook was buttering toast.
"Higgins, miss? As soon as he ate he went out. Grumbling
about having to chop at some bushes. Said Miss Coralund
asked him special or he wouldn't bother." The girl giggled.
"Higgins don't fancy work, miss, but he likes to please Miss
Coralund. She's ever so good-looking. Keep telling my
mum she looks like a film star."

Miss Sanderson hesitated, wondering if she were on the wrong track. Higgins could have wanted to please Hilary, who certainly *was* good-looking. He could have . . . only one way to find out. She retraced her steps to the foyer and donned her coat and muffler. A drone of voices came from the direction of Nurse Daley's office. The nurse and Dr. Falkner, she decided, in conference.

As she stepped out the rear door she found she needed both her heavy coat and woolen muffler. The sun was shining but the breeze was icy. She spotted Higgins trimming back the hawthorn bushes in front of the pavilion. He appeared only too willing to put down his clippers and talk. "Miss Coralund asked me yesterday to do this, miss. Soon as you took those mutts away she asked me to neaten these bushes up. Mind, if it had been one of those other trustees I wouldn't bother. But Miss Coralund doesn't order, she asks polite like. Nice lady, and for her I don't mind doing things."

Taking her cue from Hilary's technique with the surly gardener, Miss Sanderson asked politely, "Do you know anything about Tiny? Have you buried his body yet?"

"Did that last night, miss. Nurse Evans rang me up 'bout ten and asks can I come back and bury the mutt." He jerked a hand. "Got a little place down the road a bit. Not far but they got no call getting me back here at night. Told her sure but I'd be putting in for overtime. Then I come up and buried it in the corner of the kitchen garden. Whew! That beast was a weight. Had to use a wheelbarrow to move it."

"Did you see the dog after Mr. Moore locked it in your tool shed?"

He rubbed both hands down his overalls and extracted a cigarette from behind an ear. After clicking a kitchen match on a thumbnail, he held the flame to the cigarette and puffed out a cloud of smoke. "Didn't see the mutt but sure heard him. Took my hoe and shovel back to the tool shed and minute that brute heard me he started barking and howling. No way I was going to unbar that door to put the tools away. I checked the door to make sure the Great Dane weren't going to get out and left the hoe and shovel leaning against the wall. That was at quitting time—sharp five."

So, Miss Sanderson thought, at five the dog was alive and active. Maggie had mentioned the orderly had found the animal dead at around nine. Taking a deep breath, she asked the gardener the vital question. "When did you refill the hole?"

"What hole?"

"The one Tiny dug, near the sundial. You said you'd been using a shovel."

"Used the shovel to spade over the kitchen garden. Heap of work around this place in the spring and I only got one pair of hands. Didn't even think of that dog hole again. Even for Miss Coralund I couldn't see any use in filling it back in. Knew the dog would just root it up again. Beasts do that, you know. Never have liked dogs. Pee all over the place and shit on the grass and—"

"Get your shovel!"

He gave her an insolent look, butted his cigarette, and stuck the butt back behind an ear. "Don't take orders from *you* either."

Miss Sanderson found she thoroughly disliked this man. Funny, Josh's swearing had only amused her, but this man's put her back up. She stopped being polite and said crisply, "Dr. Falkner is calling in the police. You'll take orders from me or you'll be spending the next few days in the pokey. With no extra pay for overtime."

"On what charge?"

"Obstructing justice."

He cringed and went for his shovel. Miss Sanderson waited near the sundial. When he came slouching up, she told him, "Dig."

His eyes widened. "I'll be damned! Look at that. Earth put back and even the sod laid over it. Who in hell did that?"

The same person who had poisoned a dog named Tiny, Miss Sanderson said silently. Aloud, she ordered, "Dig!"

Removing the scraps of turf, he started furiously to dig. "Slower," she warned, "and carefully."

"*Women.*" He cursed softly. "Pop was right. Give them the vote and they figure they own the world. What are we digging for? Oil or water?"

She was about to respond when the gardener glanced past her and bent to his work, digging slowly and carefully. She turned. Ah, a handsome young man in a trim uniform. "P. C. Larkin," he told her, and touched a finger to his cap. "Miss Sanderson? Inspector Taylor would like a word with you."

"Soon," she said. "And I think it as well if you stay with me."

Unlike the gardener, the constable didn't argue. He looked at her and then at the excavation and stood stolidly and silently at her side. By now Higgins was thigh deep in the hole. The pile of discarded soil gradually enlarged and then Higgins stopped, bent, and leaped agilely out of the hole. "Holy Hannah! You want any more digging done, you get someone else. This is a bleeding grave!"

After shoving him to one side, the constable slid into the hole. He pointed. Miss Sanderson took two reluctant steps and followed the direction of that finger. The skull was partially masked with soil but she could see teeth grinning an ivory smile. Excellent teeth, she thought numbly, and wondered if she had seen that smile in a group photograph hanging against dull brown wainscoting. Higgins was edging away and Larkin said sharply, "You stay put. Miss

Sanderson, could you get the inspector? He's in that office behind the admittance desk."

The inspector proved to be in the middle of the foyer, deep in conversation with the doctor and nurse. He looked as young as his constable. Dr. Falkner began to make introductions but Miss Sanderson broke in. "Inspector, you'd better go to your constable."

"Where is he?"

"The sundial. Where the rose bed used to be." She swayed. "By the grave."

The doctor put an arm around her waist. "Are you all right?"

She straightened her shoulders. "No. But I will be."

"What's this about a grave?" the inspector asked.

"An old one. Perhaps thirty years old."

There were no further questions. The inspector took off at a run with Nurse Daley and Dr. Falkner at his heels. Miss Sanderson took a deep breath, loosened her coat, circled the desk, and stepped into the office behind it. The room was as neat and clean as Nurse Daley, and on a polished desk was a telephone the color of her uniform. After sinking into the swivel chair, Miss Sanderson hesitated, checked her watch, and then dialed Robby's flat. His daily answered. "He just left for chambers, Miss Sanderson. Hold the line and I'll see if I can catch him."

Miss Sanderson held the line and was rewarded with Robby's voice. He sounded breathless. "Sandy?"

She stared at a sign on the wall warning of the hazards of smoking. "You said you'd be on call."

"If you hit a snag."

"I've hit three. A dead dog, a dead nanny, the skeleton of a young man who probably was murdered thirty years ago."

The line hummed and then Forsythe asked, "Are you all right?"

She gave him the answer she'd given the inspector. "No. But I will be."

"Where will I find you?"

"I'm at the home now. Later . . . perhaps at the inn. Fiddle and Bow. Possibly at the police station."

"Hang on, Sandy. I'll try the station first."

CHAPTER 7

The police station wasn't located on the high street but, after asking directions, Forsythe found it two streets over. He drew the Rover to the curb and gazed up at a boxy modern building built of white clapboard. With the flat roof and wide windows it looked out of place among its grimy brick neighbors. Some effort to soften the stark lines had been made; window boxes, bare now, were on the upper windows, a double line of rhododendrons flanked the walk.

As he made his way up that walk, he glanced back at the cars lining the curb. There were two police cars and one brown sedan but there was no sign of Sandy's green MG. The desk sergeant, a bulky older man, assured Forsythe Miss Sanderson was indeed there, closeted with Inspector Taylor, and ushered the barrister into the inspector's office.

It was unexpectedly cozy with a pot of hyacinths perched on a windowsill and a brown teapot and mugs on a tray. Sandy was ensconced in an armchair, sipping steaming tea and nibbling biscuits. At her elbow a dark-blue tin, encircled with pictures of a royal wedding, sat.

A man rose from behind the desk, but before Forsythe took the outstretched hand, he paused at his secretary's side. The color in her face seemed to be back where it belonged, a faint tinge of rose in her thin cheeks rather than flaming red nostrils and pinkened eyelids. "You're looking better," he told her. "Is your cold gone?"

"I'd forgotten I have one. Robby, Inspector Taylor. Inspector, Robert Forsythe."

Taylor's grip was hearty and so was his voice. "A pleasure. I've heard a great deal about you, Mr. Forsythe. May I offer you tea? No. Well, as a matter of fact, I was just talking about you. Superintendent Kepesake from the C.I.D. was on the phone asking me to extend all possible courtesy to you."

"We've worked together on a few cases."

"That's what he said. He's been promoted."

"Adam was promoted about . . ."

"Six weeks ago," Miss Sanderson said.

Taylor smiled. "I do hope that sergeant of his received one too. I envy Kepesake that man."

Forsythe smiled back. "There's only one Beau. He's now not only Inspector Brummell but the father of a brand-new son."

"If anyone ever deserved a promotion, Brummell does." Taylor waved a hospitable hand. "Do take a chair, Mr. Forsythe. When Miss Sanderson called you was she able to give you any details?"

When Sandy had phoned him, the barrister thought, she had sounded deep in shock. He glanced at her, wondering if she had come out of it. She was selecting another biscuit, this one studded with bits of chocolate. "Only the bare facts. A skeleton, a dead nanny, and a dog."

Taylor's pink young face became serious. "A rotten business. It's going to take time to fill you in on the background. Miss Sanderson can handle that but I'll give you a fast sketch. We owe a great deal to your secretary. Our local physician, Dr. Falkner, was about to sign the death certificate for the dead nurse when Miss Sanderson intervened.

No discredit to the doctor. Nanny Balfour was in her late nineties, her heart was in bad condition, and it appeared she had died in her sleep. Now we believe there is good reason to believe she was smothered to death. The post-mortem will answer that but, in my own mind, I have no doubt what will be the verdict."

The inspector paused and glanced at Miss Sanderson, but she ignored him and continued sipping and nibbling. Finally he continued. "Last evening a dog belonging to one of the patients at the home was poisoned while it was locked in a tool shed at the rear of the Coralund Home. Possibly by a chunk of poisoned meat shoved through a window that had a pane broken out. This dog, a Great Dane, had been observed in the early afternoon rooting up the sod near a sundial that thirty years ago had marked the middle of a large rose garden. Thirty years ago this coming June a prominent citizen of this town disappeared—"

"He appeared to leave of his own free will," Miss Sanderson corrected.

"Right. And in this town it wasn't another nine days' wonder." Leaning back in his chair, Taylor waved a hand. "I can assure you this is a dull little place. Mainly working-class people, and the town itself rather shabby."

Forsythe nodded but he thought, More like shoddy. Taylor continued. "Nothing very exciting ever happens here and memories are long. James Coralund was a handsome young chap, about to marry a very beautiful girl, the owner of the textile plant, and reputedly well-to-do. In the years after his disappearance he and his fiancée became the basis of a legend . . . or more like a fairy tale. At the time that James Coralund disappeared I wasn't even born, but I heard the story at my mother's knee and—"

"You're a resident of the town?" Forsythe asked.

"Born and raised here. As I was saying, our parents told us the story of Hilary and Jamie, making them sound like a princess and a prince. And Hilary stayed here and she *does* look like a fairy-tale princess." Taylor gazed into space. "Lord, Hilary must be over fifty now but she still looks like a girl. Hilary Coralund, let me tell you, makes the hearts of men much her junior beat harder when they see her."

The young inspector was now looking pensively into his empty cup and Forsythe was struck with the thought that the heart under the trim gray jacket was one of those that beat hard when the fairy-tale princess hove into view. He prodded the policeman back to the present. "I gather the skeleton is that of Jamie Coralund."

"We have reason to think so. Of course, we'll have to wait for dental charts to be certain. The body—or what's left of it—was only disinterred this morning, but wheels have been turning." After flipping through a stack of papers, the inspector selected one. "Dr. Falkner is also a local. His father was the physician who attended the Coralund family. Ben Falkner went through his father's files and found that James had two bones broken. One, when the boy was eleven, was situated on the lower fibula, an inch above the ankle. When he was twelve, James snapped the trapezium bone in his left wrist. Dr. Falkner examined the bones we disinterred and has ascertained that there were breaks in the leg and arm bones in those exact spots."

"Good work," Forsythe complimented. "Could the doctor tell the cause of death?"

The inspector looked faintly pleased. "We'll have to wait on the pathologist to be sure but Ben—Doctor Falkner—found the back of the skull"—he consulted the typed sheet again—"the occipital bone was crushed. He feels death occurred as a result of a powerful blow to the back of the head."

"Were any personal effects found with the skeleton?"

"That's what clinches the whole business." The inspector leafed through the sheaf of papers. "Any number of objects, and most of them gold. If you wish, after the lab boys are finished, you can have a look at them. Ah, yes.

Here's the list. I neglected to tell you that the victim disappeared following his birthday party. He received a number of presents and some of them were in the grave—"

"How do you know this?"

"I've already spoken briefly with two of the guests at that party. Sean Ackerson and Harry Moore. I'd hoped to interview Coralund's fiancée, Hilary Coralund, but at present she's under the care of Dr. Falkner's nurse. I should imagine she's sedated. Mr. Ackerson and Mr. Moore were shocked, but they were able to tell me about the party and they remembered most of the gifts James received. Apparently the gold objects found in the grave had been gifts to him earlier that day."

Inspector Taylor cleared his throat and read, "One gold cigarette case, one gold lighter, a medallion representing Mr. Coralund's birth sign, Gemini, also made of gold and on a gold chain. All these objects were engraved with the initials JHC. A money clip made in the shape of a capital J, this given by Miss Agnes Coralund. A gold watch with a gold strap that is engraved on the back of the case with the words 'Everlasting love, Hilary.' There were also a few other things. A belt buckle, fittings from a suitcase."

Forsythe's eyes wandered from Taylor's pink young face to the purple mass of hyacinth on the sill. Death in the spring, he thought, a young man with everything to live for buried, as Egyptian pharaohs had once been entombed, surrounded by costly artifacts. "It sounds pretty conclusive," he said slowly.

"It does," Taylor agreed. "Something else survived. It's in bad shape but still identifiable. A quantity of bank notes wrapped in heavy plastic. The lab boys are working on this, and I don't know the precise amount yet but I can make a guess. Mr. Ackerson told me that after Mr. Coralund's disappearance his half sister checked his London bank account and discovered that two days before the party her brother had withdrawn one thousand pounds. At the time Miss Agnes Coralund found this reassuring, assuming the money had been used to fund her brother's departure. Have you any questions, Mr. Forsythe?"

"Dozens. But Sandy should be able to answer most of them. I would like to know if James Coralund's sister and his friends had any idea why he disappeared. It seems to me they took it rather lightly."

"He left a letter for his fiancée in the pavilion where he was staying. According to Mr. Moore, Coralund's father had had the building modernized and used it himself for the latter years of his life. After Edmund's death, his son moved into it. As an adult James wasn't often at the estate. Spent most of his time in London and—"

"The letter, Inspector."

Taylor grinned. "I am straying, aren't I? In brief, the letter stated that the writer, James Corlaund, had doubts whether the marriage he was about to enter into was a sound idea. He told Hilary he needed time to consider but did promise he'd return with his decision in a month to six weeks. And Agnes Coralund didn't take his departure lightly. After two months she reported his disappearance to the police, and after six months she hired a firm of private investigators to track down her brother. Needless to say their search was unsuccessful."

Forsythe was beginning to see why this boyish-looking man was an inspector. Taylor was not only efficient but bright. "The letter couldn't have been forged?"

"My first thought. Mr. Moore says he knows Miss Coralund has it, but he did remember the morning after the party that letter was passed around and swears the handwriting was that of James Coralund."

The barrister glanced at his secretary. Miss Sanderson had finished another biscuit and was lighting a cigarette.

He tapped long fingers against his knee. "I can guess why the Great Dane was killed. The murderer must have been afraid the dog would root up the bones. But what tie-in is there to the nanny's death—what was her name?"

"Nanny Balfour," Miss Sanderson muttered.

Inspector Taylor frowned. "At this point I can only hazard a guess. Both Dr. Falkner and Nurse Daley tell me that up to a few months ago Nanny Balfour's mind was clear as a bell. Then she started to fail and—"

"She was dozing off and talking in her sleep," Miss Sanderson said abruptly. "I visited her yesterday and right in the middle of a sentence she dozed off and started to talk to Jamie. I think someone was afraid she'd say too much." She pressed a hand to her brow. "I've just thought of something else. I don't know why it didn't occur to me before . . ."

"Shock," Taylor said sympathetically. "What have you remembered?"

"Actually it's two items. One about the dog. Apparently Tiny had an obsession about that particular spot near the sundial. Yesterday the gardener said the dog had been digging there before and—"

"How many people knew about this?"

"As far as I could tell only the gardener did. All the trustees were with me, and they seemed surprised to hear about it."

Forsythe cocked his head. "And the other item, Sandy?"

She looked not at him but at the inspector. "Did Dr. Falkner mention anything about Nanny's dreams?"

"No. Of course, we've been mainly concerned with identifying the skeleton. What dreams?"

Miss Sanderson explained about the old nurse's conviction that a "thing" had been in her room late at night on a number of occasions. Then she said bleakly, "The doctor said she was terrified and she had a weak heart."

"Hmm." Forsythe gazed from his secretary to the inspector. "It sounds as though the murderer had tried to frighten her into a heart attack."

"And failed," Taylor said grimly. "Then yesterday he or she found the dog had been repeatedly digging at the gravesite and decided it was necessary to finish off both Nanny and the Great Dane."

"Which would bring it down to the four trustees," Forsythe said.

"Not necessarily. As I said, this is a small town and news travels with the speed of light. Any number of people could have heard about the dog's digging and Nanny Balfour's dreams." The telephone pealed and Taylor made a gesture of apology as he reached for it. "Larkin? Where? Yes, right away." After pushing back his chair, he stood up. "Sorry, but I have to leave you now. But I want to assure you that you have my permission to question anyone connected with this case. In the event of objections you may use my name and I'll back you up."

"Highly irregular," Forsythe said.

The other man grinned. "You've acted as a consultant to the police before. Besides, your reputation precedes you. I welcome any help you can give. Rumors are probably flying, and with the murder of a helpless old woman feelings will be running high. The sooner we get to the bottom of this the better."

Taylor seemed to be taking his assistance for granted, Forsythe thought. The barrister looked at Miss Sanderson. "Sandy, we *are* going to investigate, aren't we?"

"We are."

"But you're the one who is always complaining about *me* dragging *you* into murder cases."

She brushed crumbs from her lap and stood up. Her pale-blue eyes coolly regarded him. "If you don't wish to become involved, go back to London. But I'm staying right here until I find the bastard who smothered an old woman and poisoned that Great Dane."

He sighed. "To do that we'll have to solve a murder that took place three decades ago."

Miss Sanderson told him, "Precisely."

Smiling broadly, the inspector said, "Looks like you're in, Mr. Forsythe."

"*We* are in," the barrister corrected.

Forsythe frowned across the table at his secretary. She was pushing food idly around her plate. "You mentioned you had no breakfast or lunch. Stop playing with your food and eat."

"I had about a dozen biscuits in the inspector's office."

"No excuses. Eat!"

"You sound exactly like Aggie. And this food is awful."

"The food is fine. Granted it's plain cooking, but the beef is excellent. So was the potato soup, and you had about one spoonful of that."

She glanced around the small dining room of the Fiddle and Bow. The only other patron was a heavyset man eating his dinner with a newspaper propped against the sugar bowl. "If the food's so great where are all the eager diners?"

He cut into a slice of rare beef. "Haven't you noticed there's a recession? I should imagine it's hit this town hard, and there may be little money for luxuries like dining out."

Her jaw set. "The bar is crowded. Oh, I know what you'll say. The same as Harry Moore. People always have money for drink."

"They seem to." Putting down his fork, he leaned forward. "You know what your problem is? You're spoiled rotten. I'll bet Aggie has been catering to your appetite, cooking little delicacies."

She broke open a roll. "Aggie is a pain in the neck but she is a marvelous cook. I do miss her cooking."

"You miss more than that. You miss Aggie."

"Robby, you may be a capable barrister and not a bad detective but you're a lousy psychoanalyst. Missing Aggie would be tantamount to missing an aching tooth."

"Admit it. You miss Aggie as much as I miss *you* when you're away."

Miss Sanderson threw down her knife. "Are you insinuating that I treat you like Aggie treats me?"

Putting out a hand, he covered one of hers. "I'm saying Aggie *cares* about you. She worries about your health, your appetite. The same way that you worry about me. Sandy, it would be a sad life if we didn't have a few friends who care."

She gave him a rueful smile. "Blimey! Do you always have to be right?"

"Always. Now, down to business. About this double murder you've pulled me into—"

"*Who* sent *who* to this town in the first place? Who said it would be a nice holiday?"

"I plead guilty, your honor. We'll have to find somewhere less public to talk, but right now I want to know this." He paused and waited until the waitress poured coffee for them. When the girl was out of earshot, he continued. "How did you get on to the nanny's death so fast? It sounded as though the doctor had no suspicion there had been foul play."

"Neither Dr. Falkner nor Nurse Daley tumbled. At first I didn't either." She stirred sugar into her cup. "The reason I was at the home this morning was to reassure two of the patients they were to keep their dogs—"

"You also made your decision on the dog issue?"

"I had, but that has no importance now. When I got to the home I found the Great Dane had been poisoned, his poor old master was laid low, and Maggie Murphy, who adores her dog, blamed *me*. Then I learned that Nanny Balfour had died during the night and her body had just been discovered. As I told you in Inspector Taylor's office,

I met the old lady yesterday and I really took a shine to her. So I went up to her room and while I was there I looked out of her window, which faces on the rear of the house. I noticed that the hole the Great Dane had dug had been filled in. The day before I'd seen the gardener, Higgins, who obviously is a lazy, shiftless fellow. Robby, my mind started to race. The dog was dead and the hole he'd been digging had been neatly filled in."

Pausing for breath, she took a sip of coffee. "I think I've been associating with you too long, Robby. I wondered if there was a connection between these current events and the disappearance of Jamie Coralund. Lord knows since I arrived in this town I've heard that name over and over again. So—"

"So you began to wonder if Nanny Balfour's death was natural?"

"And promptly found something to back my suspicions up. The medical profession is notoriously loath to be involved in ugly rumors in the case of death so I put the wind up the doctor and nurse. They called in the police and in the meantime—"

"You rooted up a skeleton." Forsythe rubbed his chin. "Sandy, do you realize that if you hadn't been on the spot all this would have worked for the person who committed the murders?"

"I should imagine it would have," she said, rather smugly.

Forsythe had been watching the waitress. She was fussing around the next table, picking up silverware and replacing it. Trying to eavesdrop? Jerking his head in her direction, he said in a low voice, "I think it better if we find that place for a private chat. Anyplace here?"

"Only Harry's office, and his wife tells me he's in there getting stinking. Not that I blame him."

"So that's why I haven't met our host. What about the Coralund Home?"

"I imagine that's where Taylor was heading, and it's probably swarming with police." She clicked a thumbnail against a front tooth and her companion winced. Then her hand dropped. "The ideal place. Near the home but not in it. Jamie's pavilion. I'll meet you outside."

"Your car or mine?"

"Have to be yours. Mine is still at the home. The inspector gave me a ride to the station." She jumped up.

He called, "Where are you going?"

"To pick up my double malt and see a man about a key."

Forsythe's Rover pulled up beside a police car. Miss Sanderson handed her employer a bottle and flipped open the glove compartment. "We'll need a flashlight, Robby." As they stepped out of the car she pointed at a brown sedan. "I was right. Inspector Taylor's car. He's working late."

"He seems a bright chap."

"Extremely sharp. Notice he said Beau Brummell deserved a promotion but didn't mention that Adam Kepesake did?"

"Beau is the *reason* Adam got his promotion. Beau always makes Adam look good. Where away?"

"Around to the back of the house. Watch your step and don't drop the booze." She flashed her light on the sundial. At the base of it a tarp covered the gaping hole. "Jamie's grave. This way, Robby."

He stumbled and caught himself. "I see what you mean about the gardener. He left a pile of branches right on the path."

"Higgins was trimming hawthorn when I more or less press-ganged his services. He's a lazy devil but in this case I'd give him the benefit of the doubt. He has probably been busy with the police." She shone the light at the door of the pavilion and pulled a key from her pocket.

"Did you get that from Moore?"

"I did. All the trustees have keys for both the home and this place." She got the door open and fumbled along the wall for a light switch. Lights sprang up in the hall and she told him, "Prepare to step back in time."

When she switched on the lights in the long living room, he could see what she meant. He shed his Burberry and wandered around, examining yellowing sheets of music, the slippers, lifting the brittle magazine. "Good Lord! This edition was published on June the second—"

"Thirty years ago. I know. Careful how you handle that. Up to now this has been the only memorial for James Hareford Coralund. That should change and the poor devil will have a proper burial and marker. How about pouring a drink, Robby?"

He glanced around. "I can see only one glass. Shall we have a loving cup?"

"There has to be another glass around. You check in here and I'll have a look in the bathroom." She picked up the glass from the desk. "Better rinse this out."

When she returned with two glasses she found Forsythe bending over the desk, pulling books from a deep lower drawer. "These go back much farther than thirty years, Sandy. These business ledgers are from the early part of the century, and a couple of letters are dated in the nineteen twenties. They once belonged to an Edmund Coralund."

"Jamie's father, and, from all accounts, devoted to wine, women, and horses."

"I believe that's song, Sandy."

"Singing wasn't mentioned."

He handed her a glass and sank down on a chair. "I must admit I'm totally at sea. Better fill me in."

"Generally or in detail?"

"Make it detail."

"Very well. Some of this is pretty dull unless you dote

on dogs. I'll begin when I arrived at the Fiddle and Bow and Harry Moore took me in hand."

In the next couple of hours, if anyone had been eavesdropping, he would have been gaping in amazement. Abigail Sanderson's mind was often compared to a computer and her memory rivaled any machine built. She was able to recount events and conversations verbatim. Her employer's concentration was as amazing. He sat quietly and seldom interrupted. Finally she finished, rubbed her throat, and rose to replenish their glasses. "Compliments are in order, Robby."

"Consider them proffered. You know, Sandy, by some you might be considered a freak. Practically a photographic memory."

"Much easier than taking notes. Now, maestro, any ideas stirring?"

"Early on yet. We'll have to burrow into the memories of the guests at that birthday party. There were eight people there."

"Nine. Don't forget Nanny Balfour. Probably she's the one who took that group photograph."

He drummed his fingers against his knee. "I don't see a copy here."

She glanced at the silver frames glinting in the lamplight. "Not in evidence anyway. But not to worry. I understand all the trustees have a copy. Harry has one in his office. One of the members of that party is now in California and may be eliminated. Agnes Coralund could hardly have sneaked around poisoning a dog. That leaves the four surviving members of the Gang and the two hangers-on —the vicar and his wife." Draining her glass, she rose. "Three for each of us. Any you fancy?"

He glanced at one of the silver frames. "I think I'd better delve into Hilary's memory banks."

"You are not delving into anything connected with Hilary Coralund. I'll handle her."

"Madly sexy, is she? Might cloud my judgment?"

Miss Sanderson shot him a disdainful look. "Getting your exercise jumping to conclusions, are you? Hilary is *not* sexy. Granted she has a devastating effect on men. I could see it working on young Dr. Falkner, and our good inspector had a glint in his eyes when he talked about Princess Hilary. Even that ape Higgins has fallen under her spell."

"Sounds like she's a witch."

"Not that either. Hilary's appeal stems from beauty and gentleness and an aura of silent suffering. A fatal combination to the male beast. Brings out their chivalry."

He grinned. "Have you selected your other victims?"

"Mr. and Mrs. Andrew Parker. The vicar and his mate."

"Which leaves me the other trustees. All men so I shouldn't have to strain my chivalry." He helped her on with her coat. "We'll get started tomorrow. A word of caution. Watch yourself."

"Are you hinting . . ."

"I'm hinting that if Miss Sanderson had not been in this town our killer would be safe. He or she may not take kindly to having you digging up the past. And I do know this. This individual moves quickly and decisively and cunningly."

He held the flashlight while she locked the door behind them. As she turned the circle of light moved across her face. "Take your own advice, Robby. You too will be digging up the dirt and as Inspector Taylor mentioned, your reputation always precedes you."

"I'll keep that in mind," he said gravely.

CHAPTER 8

The public library was on the same street as the police station and looked about the same age as the inn where Forsythe had spent the night. Its brick was begrimed with decades of soot and the building had an air of neglect. The interior proved to be a shock. Grids of fluorescent lamps cast a stark white glare and the desk was modern and built of steel. The girl behind that desk was also up-to-date. A sweater strained over large, shapely, unfettered breasts, her hair fell in a friz to her shoulders, her mouth was heavy with gleaming scarlet. As she gave him a welcoming smile, he noted a smudge of lip rouge on a front tooth.

"Mr. Dorf? Yes, Lee came to work this morning. I didn't really expect him. Such a shock, you know. I mean, an old friend found like that. Poor dear! He's back in the stacks somewhere."

Forsythe waited for her to leave her post to find the librarian. He was rather interested in whether the rest of her body measured up to that splendid chest. He was to be disappointed. Throwing back her head, she shouted, "Lee! Someone to see you."

Her summons brought not one man but two. The older, clutching a newspaper, merely stuck a balding head around a bookcase and then withdrew it. The other man made for the desk. He didn't hurry and he didn't offer his hand. "Mr. Forsythe? Yes, I've been expecting you. But hardly this early."

"Has Inspector Taylor been in touch?"

"He rang me up last evening." Dorf glanced at his assistant. She was leaning forward, her eyes avid, her lips drawn back exposing the smeared tooth. With an expression of distaste, he told her, "If you need me, we'll be in my office. And you know better than to yell like that. It disturbs the patrons."

"Sorry, Lee, I keep forgetting. Can I get something, Lee? You know, like a nice cuppa. I mean—"

"No. Mr. Forsythe, this way." Dorf led the way between ranks of books toward the rear of the building. Opening a door, he ushered Forsythe into a barren room. It looked as shabby as Dorf's blue suit. "The help we have to put up with now! A nice cuppa! What Cindy means is that she'd like to overhear a few tidbits to pass on to her friends."

"Aren't you being rather harsh? In a town this size there's bound to be interest—"

"Use the right term. Vulgar and vicious curiosity." As though suddenly exhausted, Dorf sank into the chair behind the desk. He made no offer of a chair for the other man but Forsythe drew one up. As Miss Sanderson had, he noticed the weariness of the deep-set eyes. Passing a hand over those eyes, Dorf muttered, "You must excuse my behavior. Last night I didn't get any sleep. And yet, in an odd way, I feel relieved. Something has been finalized. I hope now Hilary will be able to get on with a normal life. That we'll all be able to get on."

Forsythe studied the older man. If it weren't for the misshapen nose Leroy Dorf, even in his fifties, would have been a fine-looking man. He thought of reaching for his pipe, noticed a large sign on the far wall forbidding this, considered reaching for his notebook and pen, and decided against it. Instead, he asked, "Did you, like Mr. Moore and Mr. Ackerson, believe that James Coralund was dead?"

"I see Miss Sanderson has filled you in. I suppose she would. You act as a team, don't you? Yes, Mr. Forsythe, for many years I've had to accept the fact that Jamie was dead. We couldn't convince Hilary of this." He pushed back the lock of hair from his left temple and Forsythe caught a glimpse of an ugly scar that ran up into the hairline. A pity. The brow was well shaped and wide. "Well, you might as well start your third degree."

"Hardly that. But to discover the person who killed your friend we must search your memories. I will tell you this. On my way here I stopped to speak with Inspector Taylor. The autopsy has been completed and Nanny Balfour died from asphyxiation, probably suffocated with her pillow."

The weary eyes closed. "Poor dear Nanny Balfour. What a foul act! I'll do my best to help. Now, where to start . . ."

"Perhaps with your friendship with James Coralund."

"That goes back half a century. When I was first taken to the Coralund manor to keep Jamie company I was only five. His sister, Agnes, was a grown woman, well on the way to spinsterhood, when he was born, and his childhood had been a lonely one."

"I understand he did have his small cousin with him."

"Jamie's father had sent for Hilary when she was orphaned, but she was younger than Jamie and a girl. Edmund Coralund was determined to buy playmates for his son—"

"Buy?"

"Like a baron bringing in sons of his serfs to amuse his heir. Edmund bought three little boys, all the same age as his son. Sean Ackerson's mother ran a notion shop and she barely scraped along. Harry's dad and mother had the Fiddle and Bow but were far from prosperous. I was the poorest of the lot. My parents had a few acres outside of town where we eked out an existence. We raised vegetables and had hens and a couple of cows. Mother did most of the work and sold produce door to door and my father did a few odd jobs."

Dorf's slender fingers spun a merry-go-round of rubber stamps. "You'll hear all about my father so I might as well be candid. Amos Dorf was the town drunk. When I was not quite sixteen he died. When he was sober he wasn't too bad, but alcohol turned him into a beast. He abused my mother and shortened her life and he hated me as much as I did him. While Mother was alive she shielded me, but shortly before my ninth birthday she died. A combination of overwork and ill treatment. Then Amos Dorf turned all his venom on me."

The librarian's fingers left the stamps and he touched his nose, pulled back the graying hair from the red scar on his brow, and he said grimly, "The day after Mother's funeral he beat me nearly to death. These are my inheritances from Amos Dorf. He left me unconscious in my room, didn't even bother calling a doctor. Jamie and Harry came out to see me and they went immediately to Jamie's dad. The upshot was that Edmund Coralund arrived like an avenging fury. Used his riding crop on Amos and then he took me to old Dr. Falkner to be patched up. I was hoping Edmund wouldn't send me back to the farm but that's what he did."

The barrister was frowning. "I understand you did live at the Coralund manor."

"When my father finally drank himself to death Edmund took me in. Our little farm was heavily mortgaged and there was no money. So I lived at the manor on Edmund's charity. But I must admit that Amos never beat me again. Oh, he'd slap me around but he never beat me. The only man Amos Dorf feared was Edmund Coralund."

"But up to that time you did visit Jamie's home."

"As Nanny used to say, the three of us practically lived

there. That was the only thing that made my life bearable. Playing with Jamie's toys, eating the delicious food Nanny prepared for us . . . it was heaven, but then I'd have to return to my father and hell."

"I sense you feel no gratitude to Edmund."

"Not a whit. Edmund distributed largess with a generous hand, but when a person has as much as he did that isn't a sacrifice. And he got what he paid for—Jamie had his three small slaves."

"Did you dislike Jamie too?"

The older man's face suddenly brightened with a warm smile. "I thought the world of Jamie. Harry always says we were like planets revolving around the sun. And he's right. Jamie was the light, the warmth, in our lives. He was a Gemini and, true to his birthsign, had two sides. He liked his own way and when his mind was truly made up he couldn't be budged. But Nanny handled him with a firm hand and he didn't lord it over Harry and Sean and me."

"Tell me more about Jamie's father."

Dorf's eyes narrowed and he tugged a sleeve down over a frayed shirt cuff. "I fail to see what this has to do with Jamie's murder. Edmund died from a stroke almost five years before Jamie disappeared."

"Background is sometimes important."

Leaning back in his chair, Dorf stroked his tapered chin. "I can tell you about one incident that will show you exactly the kind of man Edmund was. It was my eighteenth birthday and it was in the last week of May. I'm about three weeks older than Jamie was. A few months before Edmund had suffered a slight stroke, but he was recovering and announced that as my present he was treating Jamie and me to a night on the town. We thought he meant this town, but Edmund took us to London and we were thrilled. Jamie and I assumed he was giving us a lavish dinner and afterward we would be attending the theater. We were right about the meal but . . ."

Dorf's voice trailed off but Forsythe didn't prod the other man. Then the deep-set eyes turned to the barrister. "Do you know where that scoundrel took two boys still in their teens?" The question appeared to be rhetorical as he hurried on. "To a house of ill repute! A foul place where they sold female flesh like a . . . a butcher shop. Edmund was well acquainted with it and the fat old hag who ran it. He called her Belle and she hugged and kissed him. He told her to go easy, he was recovering from a stroke and his sporting days were over, but he had a couple of likely lads to be broken in. He picked out the women himself, not young ones but raddled harlots. One was a bleached blonde, the other with hair dyed the color of Maggie Murphy's. They both wore dressing gowns, none too clean, and the fronts gaped open so you could see their . . . everything they had."

Leroy Dorf's description was so vivid that Forsythe could see the scene. Two slender blond boys, embarrassed and shy, being pulled upstairs by a couple of ladies of the evening while Edmund sipped champagne and joked with the madam of the house.

Jamie and Lee were taken to a room with a huge bed and the women started kissing and fondling them, trying to loosen their clothes. Lee fended the blonde off and looked, as he always did, for Jamie to extricate them. And Jamie did.

"Jamie received a good-size allowance," Dorf explained. "I begged him to pay those women off so they'd leave us alone but he said it wouldn't work, they'd take the money and talk anyway. His father would hear and then all hell would break loose. Then Jamie winked at me and told the women, 'Play cards or do whatever you do when you're not working. And when we go downstairs don't you say a word about what happened in this room.' The redhead laughed and said, 'You mean what *didn't* happen!' Then Jamie got an ugly look on his face and he said, 'You open

your filthy mouths and I'll tell my father you made us—'
and he leaned over and whispered. Both the women looked
scared to death, and when Jamie came back over I asked
him what he'd whispered. He laughed and said his father
hated perversion and he'd mentioned something so per-
verse Edmund would hit the roof."

Dorf paused and his lips curved into a smile. "It worked
too. When we went downstairs Edmund asked how his boys
had performed and the women told him we were 'randy
young studs.' That pleased him, and he roared with laughter and thumped Jamie's and my shoulder." The smile
vanished and the man's mouth twisted with disgust. "That
was Edmund Coralund. When he had another stroke three
years later and died I was glad. Somehow I think Jamie
was relieved too. His father had insisted Jamie stay at home
and learn the family business, and Jamie wasn't interested
in it. After Edmund's death Jamie was free to go to London
and do what *he* wanted, study music. Edmund had left me
a little legacy and I went with Jamie. We shared a flat that
the Coralunds kept there, and Jamie took lessons and I
wrote poetry."

The barrister studied the older man. A singularly cold
chap, showing not one trace of gratitude toward the man
who not only opened the doors of his house to him but
also provided for him in his will. After clearing his throat,
he said, "Would you tell me about the birthday party. That
was in June, wasn't it?"

"June the fifteenth. A Saturday. Agnes had arranged it
and had invited all the members of the Gang as well as
Joanne Drew and Andy Parker. We were to have a festive
day and spend the night at the manor. At the time Joanne
was working in London, and Jamie and I gave her a ride
down with us. From the beginning I sensed it was going
to be a flop. We arrived around ten in the morning and I
could tell Agnes and Hilary had had words—"

"How did Jamie's sister and his fiancée get along?"

"I never had the impression they really liked each other but generally they covered up their feelings. That day they were making little effort. To add to the occasion Nanny Balfour was out of sorts. She was in the midst of a bout of sciatica and was hobbling around and being grouchy."

"It doesn't sound as though the day began well."

"It got off to an awful start, but by the time the birthday dinner was served things seemed a trifle more harmonious. Agnes had arranged the dinner be held at noon as she'd given the servants the rest of the day and that night off. The food was tasty and there was a huge cake with a white piano on the top. After Jamie blew out the candles and sliced the cake, his gifts were presented. Then all hell broke loose. Not only would he not put on Hilary's gift immediately—she'd given him a gold watch—but he kissed Joanne after he opened her gift. Hilary was always green-eyed with jealousy, and she had the idea Joanne was trying to take Jamie away from her.

"Nanny and I managed to soothe Hilary, and Agnes suggested tennis. We decided to play mixed doubles. Jamie choose Joanne as his partner. Hilary and I played against them and we lost. Jamie kissed Joanne again and Hilary stalked off in tears. Then Nanny threw up her hands, said we were all naughty children, and took herself off to her room. I was wishing I could do the same."

Forsythe sat forward. "When was the group photograph taken?"

"After dinner, just before we started to play tennis. I have my copy here. Would you like to see it?"

"Very much."

After fishing in his pocket, Dorf extracted a ring of keys, selected one, and bent to unlock a lower drawer. He took out a framed photo and handed it across the desk. "Nanny Balfour took this. I can remember her ordering everyone to smile."

"I can see one person who didn't obey."

"Andy Parker? He was glum all day. Not that the poor chap had much to smile about. He must have felt like a fish out of water. Agnes made it quite clear the only reason he'd been invited was because of Joanne. And poor Andy couldn't play tennis and so he had to sit and watch. Andy was as jealous as Hilary was and didn't care for Jamie's attentions to Joanne."

Forsythe handed the picture back and his companion replaced it in the drawer and relocked it. "Could you fill in the rest of that day, Mr. Dorf?"

"The rest of the day . . . Well, after Hilary and Nanny left the rest of us continued to play tennis to put in the time until supper. Sean and I were fair players and Jamie was very good but Harry was the star. He always excelled at sports. Andy Parker sat and glowered and Joanne made up to Jamie. Finally Agnes rooted out Hilary to help her prepare a cold meal, and afterward we were supposed to have a musical evening. Jamie was to play the piano and Hilary and I were to sing. I had a fair tenor and Hilary has a lovely contralto. But as soon as supper was finished, around ten I think, Jamie said he was tired and was calling it a day. He said good night and headed down to the pavilion. Harry and Sean and I tagged along to get a breath of air. Jamie didn't ask us in, he just turned and waved from the doorway. That was the last time any of us saw him."

Not quite, Forsythe thought. One of them must have seen Coralund later. The murderer. Aloud he asked, "What did you do then?"

Dorf gave him a wry smile. "My alibi? The night was cool so the three of us wandered back to the manor. Sean and Harry went to the billiard room and I went directly upstairs—"

"Where were the rest of the guests?"

Dorf thought for a moment. "I have no idea. I would imagine Hilary and Agnes were in the kitchen. Andy and

Joanne . . . possibly they'd gone up to their rooms. All I
know is that I went up to mine, read for a time, and then
went to sleep. I do remember thinking I should be glad
to leave for London in the morning. Jamie wasn't leaving
with me. The wedding was planned for the following Fri-
day and I'd be back for that. Any further questions?"

"A few. I understand Jamie was contemplating setting
up the home for the aged. When did he mention this?"

"Let me think. Some of this is so hazy. I believe he first
mentioned it at dinner. But he talked about it off and on
for the rest of the day. Made Agnes unhappy and upset
Hilary even more. But once Jamie had his teeth in an idea
he was impossible to divert."

"His treatment of his fiancée—a strange way to act with
the girl he was soon to marry."

"You must realize that Hilary was more eager for that
marriage than Jamie was. He might have felt trapped."
Dorf stroked his delicate chin. "From the time I can remember Edmund and Marion Coralund took for granted
that Jamie and his cousin would eventually marry. But they
weren't formally engaged until shortly before Marion's
death. She died in February and Jamie gave Hilary the
ring in late January. Under pressure from his dying
mother, I would imagine. Odd . . . Hilary could have had
her choice of so many men. Sean and Harry were wild for
her and me . . . I've adored her since we were children.
But Hilary had her heart set on Jamie."

"I understand the three of you still look after her."

"We do our best. Sean ferries her around in his car and
gives her expensive presents. Harry, as he says, when she
crooks her finger he comes running. I have no funds for
a car or presents but I do have a rented cottage near where
she lives, and I do her gardening and odd jobs and most
of her shopping." Dorf smiled crookedly. "Hilary still loves
Jamie and we still love her." He pulled his long frame up.
"I'll walk you to the door, Mr. Forsythe."

After opening the door, Forsythe followed the librarian down a narrow aisle. "Isn't it rather awkward without a car?"

Dorf shrugged. "At times. But my cottage is within walking distance of this library."

"You do go out to the home often."

"Sometimes Sean gives me a lift or Harry picks me up in his van. The home is about a mile from my cottage, and quite often I walk."

They were moving past the desk and Cindy raised her frizzed head to give Dorf an enticing smile. Dorf ignored her but the barrister noticed that either the lip rouge had been removed from her tooth or had worn off. It made a definite improvement in her appearance. Forsythe thanked Leroy Dorf and this time the man extended a hand.

As the barrister returned to his car he was aware that Dorf still stood in the doorway. After getting behind the wheel, Forsythe pulled out his pipe and proceeded to load it with dark, fragrant tobacco. The door of the library closed with a thud.

CHAPTER 9

Shortly after Leroy Dorf ushered Forsythe into his office, Miss Sanderson's green MG pulled to a stop in front of the Parkers' house. She made no effort to get out of the car but sat studying the vicarage. She had been born in a small-town vicarage and had lived her first seven years there. Her home had been a large, sprawling house, but hardly spacious enough to shelter the numerous young Sandersons. As she often mentioned to Robby, her father had had more children than income and when a childless aunt offered to raise little Abigail and educate her, that offer had been accepted with muted but genuine relief.

Abigail Sanderson sometimes wondered why Aunt Rose had selected *her*. She had been the thinnest and homeliest of the Sanderson girls. All her sisters had been nicer looking, and Teresa had been a beauty. Whatever the reason for Aunt Rose's choice, the result was that Abigail had been raised with all the privileges and some of the loneliness of an only child.

The Parker vicarage brought back no nostalgic yearnings. They lived in a compact stone cottage. The door was painted apple green and the curtains in the small front windows were a similar shade. She gathered together her muffler and handbag and made her way up to the green door. In a border beside the steps snowdrops were pushing pallid heads through leaf mold and the bush near them was budding with tiny leaves almost the color of the door. She decided that later in the season the tiny garden plot would be colorful and cheerful.

The woman who opened the door was also colorful and cheerful. Slender Joanne Drew had blossomed into a matronly figure, the pretty face puffed with round pink cheeks and a series of extra chins. A peasant blouse and a full cotton skirt fairly bulged, but she had a pleasant smile and fine dark eyes. "Miss Sanderson. You really shouldn't have troubled to phone ahead."

"I thought it only courteous, Mrs. Parker." Miss Sanderson surrendered her coat and muffler and followed a beckoning hand into a crowded sitting room. As she glanced around, nostalgia stirred. This was a room that brought back memories of her mother's cluttered parlor, but instead of stuffed toys and dolls and puzzles the Parkers' sitting room was littered with untidy stacks of newspapers, magazines, a workbox spilling mending.

Joanne Parker's laugh was as pleasant as her smile. "You see what I meant? If I hadn't known you were coming I could have found an excuse for this muddle. I really am a terrible housekeeper." She swept a heap of magazines from an armchair. "But do be seated and ignore the mess. May I offer you refreshment? Coffee, perhaps?"

"Thank you, no." Miss Sanderson returned her hostess's smile. "This room takes me back to the home I remember as a child. My father was vicar in a small town."

"Then you understand. The wives of vicars have so little time to tend to their own homes. I seem to do nothing but run from one meeting to another."

"I do hope I haven't interrupted your work."

The round face sobered and Joanne Parker sagged into the corner of a couch. "I canceled my meetings for today. That dreadful business with Jamie and then Nanny Balfour . . . My husband is on the phone now trying to locate someone who knows what arrangements will be made. For funeral services, you know. I understand you are representing Agnes Coralund. Would you know what she wishes in regard to her brother's . . . remains?"

"No, but my employer will be contacting her. I should imagine Miss Coralund will wish a memorial service, but I doubt she'll be able to attend herself."

"Agnes must be—heavens, she must be eighty now. She was such a strong, vital person it's hard to picture her aging."

Miss Sanderson fumbled in her handbag for cigarettes and then hastily withdrew her hand. It was possible the Parkers shared the dislike so many people did for nicotine. The fine dark eyes followed the movement, and Mrs. Parker jumped up in a swirl of bright cotton and produced a heavy glass ashtray. The bottom was decorated with an advertisement for the Fiddle and Bow. "Do smoke if you wish. Andy—my husband—loves his pipe. I don't smoke myself but have no objection to other people smoking."

Miss Sanderson selected a cigarette and clicked her lighter. She wondered how to begin. She soon found there was no need to explain the reason for her visit. "Inspector Taylor has been in touch with us," Mrs. Parker told her. "Andy and I know how difficult this must be for you. You may feel you're prying. But I assure you Andy and I are anxious to get to the bottom of this dreadful affair. It casts a pall over this town. To think someone we may call a friend, someone we see frequently, who may come to our church services—well, you must understand our feelings."

"I do." Miss Sanderson tapped ash into the ashtray and asked, "You and your husband were friends of Jamie Coralund when you were children, weren't you?"

"Hardly friends. We knew him, of course. But there was

a wide gulf between the Coralunds and our parents. My dad had a tiny greengrocery and Andy's father was a carpenter. Sean and Harry and Lee came from similar backgrounds but Edmund Coralund, Jamie's father, had given them open sesame to the manor. Andy and I did try to join their gang but to no avail. It was a magical circle and we weren't welcome."

"And yet you were at Jamie's last birthday party."

"Indeed we were. I was in my early twenties before I came to really know Jamie. I'd taken a position as clerk in a dress shop in London—" Mrs. Parker paused and smiled again. "Such a silly girl! I couldn't wait to leave this town. I thought life here was so dull and monotonous, and I pictured myself leading a glamorous life in the big city. It didn't work that way. All I had in London was a dull little room, a dull little job, and not one person to call a friend. I was desperately lonely and finally rang up Jamie. He and Lee Dorf were sharing a flat there. I was so nervous when I did it but Jamie was wonderful! He took me out for dinner and—"

"You never told me about this," a deep and rather oily voice announced.

Mrs. Parker turned her head. "For a good reason. When we were young you were so foolishly jealous. Miss Sanderson, my husband."

"And a husband no longer young but still jealous," the vicar told Miss Sanderson. He gave her a hearty handshake and sat down close to his wife.

Andrew Parker hadn't changed as much as his wife had. His hair was thinner and the wispy remains were brushed across a gleaming skull, but his face was plump and he wore a jolly smile. "While we're reminiscing, Joannie, let me remind you that at one time your interest in Jamie Coralund nearly drove me wild. He was such a handsome chap—But tell us more of how wonderful Jamie was to you in London."

"It was all quite innocent, Andy. Jamie merely felt sorry for me and treated me to a few dinners, and once he took me with him to a pub that artists frequented. Lee Dorf was with us and I've always remembered that evening. We drank wine and all the young men were so eager and alive and talking at the tops of their voices. About poetry and music and their dreams. I couldn't really understand what they were saying, but I loved sitting beside Jamie—"

"And dreaming one day you might be Mrs. Jamie Coralund."

He *is* jealous, Miss Sanderson thought. He's keeping that smile in place but is still passionately jealous of a man who has been dead for three decades. The vicar glanced at her and his smile wavered. "You mustn't think me callous, teasing my wife this way. I do feel badly about the manner of Nanny Balfour's death, but I scarcely knew young Coralund. The only time I was ever at the manor was for the birthday party, and when Agnes invited me I had the notion it was simply to provide another guest. I went because Joannie would be there, but when she arrived with Jamie and Lee she ignored me."

His wife squeezed his plump arm. "You silly old thing. Married for over a quarter of a century and still remembering what a silly girl did to you so long ago. I'll admit I was infatuated with Jamie. And I never had the impression he genuinely loved Hilary. Oh, I know they were engaged, but look how he treated her that day."

"Yes, quite shabbily. He gave most of his attention to you. Even kissed you twice. Once—"

"Ah, yes. When Jamie opened that cheap tie I'd brought for him. But that was only because I felt so badly when I saw all the expensive gifts he'd been given. Jamie was so sensitive. He was only trying to make me feel better."

"He certainly succeeded. You lit up like a light bulb."

The Parkers seemed to have forgotten Miss Sanderson

but she didn't mind. She might learn more this way than with questioning. Mrs. Parker touched her lips with a tender finger as though she could still feel the warmth of Jamie Coralund's lips lingering there. "I was shocked, Andy. Hilary was looking daggers but Agnes didn't seem disturbed. Neither did Nanny Balfour. Really, I expected her to chide Jamie. She was so forthright and she had raised Hilary from the time the girl was a baby."

"I've heard that Nanny always made it clear that Jamie was her favorite. That was common talk in town. But after the tennis set when Jamie kissed and hugged you again I felt like knocking him down!"

Mrs. Parker gave a pleased, girlish giggle. "How gallant, dear! But Jamie was only excited about our winning the game. Hilary was such a good player, so strong and athletic, and so was Lee Dorf. I couldn't play well and I suppose Jamie didn't think we had a chance."

"You played as though you were inspired. And you looked so pretty in that short white dress." His eyes left his wife's round face and fastened on Miss Sanderson. "We've been rambling on, Joannie, and being rude to our guest. Have you offered Miss Sanderson refreshment?"

"Coffee. Miss Sanderson didn't care for it."

"I agree with her. We'll have a drop of sherry." As he bustled around, he told Miss Sanderson, "Dreadfully early for this sort of thing but this is an unusual and upsetting day."

She watched him as he poured. His rotund body was attired in an old sweater with leather-patched elbows, baggy twill pants, and a plaid shirt. She sipped and found his sherry was excellent.

"Perhaps, Miss Sanderson, you'd like to ask questions."

"I take it the atmosphere at the birthday party wasn't exactly pleasant."

"Unpleasant enough that if it hadn't been for Joannie

I'd have left. I can tell you I wasn't looking forward to spending the night in that house. Everyone seemed at loggerheads. Sean and Harry weren't getting along, Nanny was miserable with sciatica, Jamie and Hilary were on the edge of a quarrel, and to top if off Agnes and Hilary weren't hitting it off."

"And you were annoyed at your wife."

"Future wife. Joannie and I were married after Jamie had been gone for about three years. I suppose by that time she'd given up hope of him coming back."

"Andy! It wasn't like that and you know it!" Mrs. Parker slammed down her glass. "I knew at the time there was no hope of Jamie breaking off with his fiancée. Hilary was such a beautiful creature and she had wonderful clothes and jewelry. And I understood both Jamie's mother and father doted on her, considered her a daughter. And yet . . . it seemed to me that Jamie didn't really want to marry her."

"I sensed that too." This time the vicar was gazing at his guest. "I've often thought that perhaps Jamie loved Hilary like a brother, not like a fiancé. They looked so much alike, maybe he felt like her brother."

"Could you tell me more about that day? Anything you remember might be helpful."

They told her about the day. Sometimes they spoke at the same time and they continually interrupted each other. "The servants left immediately after they'd served the birthday dinner," Mrs. Parker recalled. "I had the notion that that was what was responsible for the coldness between Hilary and Agnes. They had to do the domestic work, and Hilary hated housework. Supper was a disappointment. I'd expected another meal like dinner, something lavish, but we were served cold food buffet style. Salads and cold cuts. Pork and beef—"

"And chicken," her husband said. "The only hot food was buns, and dessert was a fruit salad."

Miss Sanderson had no interest in that menu. Moving restlessly, she said, "And after supper was over?"

"Everything fell flat," the vicar said. "We'd been told there was to be a musical evening and—"

"It sounded so exciting," his wife said. "Jamie had written musical scores for some of Lee's poems and I was looking forward to hearing them performed. But Jamie jumped up, said he was tired, and was off to bed. Really quite rude." Mrs. Parker's full lips pouted. "He left for his pavilion and the rest of us just stood there, looking at each other. Jamie's three friends followed him out and Agnes told Hilary they might as well clean up the kitchen. I went to the kitchen to offer to help but Agnes told me not to bother and Hilary turned her back on me. Then—"

"I'd waited for Joannie at the foot of the staircase. She came bolting down the hall looking angry and flushed—"

"Hilary had deliberately snubbed me, Andy. Of course I was annoyed. We went up together and Andy walked me to my room—"

"Which was right beside the one I was in. I didn't sleep well and the following morning—"

"Did those rooms overlook the rear garden?" Miss Sanderson asked.

He shook his head. "As far as I know the only rooms that overlooked that area were the servants' quarters and the nursery and Nanny Balfour's room. As I started to say, the following morning when I went down to the breakfast room I found the household in an uproar. No breakfast had been prepared and Hilary was on the brink of tears again."

His wife nodded and her chins waggled. "During the night Jamie had left the estate—"

"Appeared to have left," her husband said gloomily.

"Hindsight, Andy. At that time we believed he had

left. And Hilary had a letter he'd written to her. When I came down Agnes was reading it and then it was handed around. Hilary was in an awful shape, and Nanny put her arms around the poor girl and told her that Jamie had promised to come back and he always kept his promises. Andy whispered that he thought it only polite to leave and so we did. Later that day I took a train back to London."

"This letter," Miss Sanderson said. "It was in Jamie's writing, was it?"

"I've no idea. I wasn't shown it," the vicar said. "I'd never seen his handwriting anyway. But no one questioned it."

"Jamie wrote me a couple of notes," Mrs. Parker said. "I only had a quick look at the letter but I'd say it was the same writing. But I have no doubt that Hilary still has that letter."

Miss Sanderson had no doubts on that score either. She lit a cigarette. "How do you get along with Hilary now, Mrs. Parker?"

"We have a good relationship. Both of us mellowed with the years. And Hilary is much nicer now than she was when we were young. We've worked together for the home for the aged for many years. Strange what changes time makes in people. When I was a girl I felt nothing but dislike and envy for Hilary and now . . . I pity the poor thing."

"As a Christian, you should," her husband told her rather pompously. "All those people seemed to have so much when we had very little. They were bright and talented and their futures looked so hopeful. But look at them now."

She reached for his hand and squeezed it. "And we've had so much, dear. Our church, our work, each other."

Miss Sanderson had looked in vain for photographs of their family. She said slowly, "I suppose your children are grown up."

"Alas, Miss Sanderson, the dear Lord never blessed Joannie and me with children."

"We both love children, Miss Sanderson, but I was unable to have any. An operation when I was barely seventeen . . ."

Her husband put an arm around her shoulders. "A tragedy, but no need to go into that. God did give us each other. Think of the blessings we do have."

Her dark eyes were misty but she managed a smile. "The person I feel most sorry for is Lee Dorf. He's such a sad man. All he has is that job at the library and the work he does for the home. Living all alone in that dreary little cottage."

"Joannie, if Lee wanted he could have more than that."

"Cindy Hall? Yes, I've heard she is taken with Lee." Miss Sanderson lifted a brow and Mrs. Parker explained. "Cindy is Lee's assistant at the library. Very pretty but so young."

"It might work out. Perhaps Lee will . . ." Mr. Parker's voice trailed away. "I feel sorry for Sean Ackerson too."

"Sean's a wealthy man, Andy. His shop and that car and—"

"Wealth can never buy what we most desire." Clearing his throat, he glanced at the mantel clock. "Nearly lunchtime. Miss Sanderson, you must have luncheon with us. Joannie is a fine cook."

His wife beamed. "Much better at cooking than at housework. Andy, do give Miss Sanderson a bit more sherry. We won't take no for an answer, my dear."

Miss Sanderson politely protested but to no avail. She had another excellent sherry and, in time, an excellent lunch. Her appetite proved robust, her hosts cheerful, and when she left the vicarage the sun was beaming warmth down.

A promising day, she told herself, as she drove in the direction of Hilary Coralund's cottage.

CHAPTER 10

Sunlight was streaming through the windows of the public bar of the Fiddle and Bow. Forsythe paused in the doorway, looking for his secretary. Business wasn't brisk. There were only two young chaps in jeans and T-shirts playing darts and a couple of older men engrossed in a game of draughts. Mrs. Moore was behind the counter polishing glasses. She glanced up and beckoned to him. "Mrs. Parker left a message for you, sir. Said to tell you Miss Sanderson is taking lunch at the vicarage." She sniffed. "Hope your secretary likes their food better than *mine*."

Time for diplomacy, Forsythe decided. "I've certainly done justice to your cooking, Mrs. Moore. As for Sandy—colds do put one off. Speaking of food, I think I'll have a pint and one of those delicious meat pies. Pork?"

"Beef. Care for a bit of salad and some bread and cheese?"

Forsythe did and waited at the bar for his lunch. As Mrs. Moore drew his pint, he asked. "Would it be possible to speak to your husband this afternoon?"

She hesitated and lowered her voice. "Harry's in bad shape. Drank half the night and I had to put him to bed. Now, don't get the idea my Harry's a heavy drinker, Mr. Forsythe. Usually only has a pint or a nip of brandy, but

that business at the home has hit him awful hard. He
thought the world of Nanny Balfour and then that Coralund man . . . it's dreadful!"

"It is indeed. Not to worry, Mrs. Moore, there's no rush
to talk to your husband. I'll catch him when he's feeling
better."

"Good of you, sir." She handed him a stein. "Nell—she's
our barmaid—said she saw you going into the library this
morning. How's Lee Dorf taking it?"

"He's looking drawn and tired. He said he didn't sleep
last night."

"So sad. Wonder how Miss Coralund is." Her lips
twitched in a bitter little smile. "Least she hasn't yelled for
Harry."

He picked up his plate. "Were you raised here, Mrs.
Moore?"

She shook her head. "Came from Manchester. Met my
Harry there when he was still playing football. The first
time he asked me out I couldn't believe my ears. Harry
was a fine footballer and the girls went wild for him. Always
trailing around after him and asking for autographs.

"A shame he had the hip injury. But Harry's a cheerful
man and he did have this inn to fall back on. The Fiddle
and Bow has been in the Moore family a long time. My
Harry's kind of hoping one of our boys will take it over
when we get too old to carry on. But our older son, Alan,
is doing well in sales, and young Harry is an accountant.
Can't expect them to drop everything and tend bar."

Forsythe started toward a table and then turned back to
the bar. Mrs. Moore was drawing a pint for one of the dart
players, and he waited until the young chap had been
served. "Mrs. Moore, can you tell me where I can find Mr.
Ackerson?"

"At his shop. Sean has rooms behind it. It's up the street
from here. You won't have any trouble spotting it. Best-

looking shop on the high street. Sean had the brick sand-
blasted and put in fancy windows."

With this description Forsythe had no trouble finding
the shop. It stood out in pristine splendor between its
shabby neighbors. The windows were bowed with leaded
panes. On the door tiny gold letters whispered that this
was the home of Ackerson's Fine Antiques. Fine is right,
he thought, looking at two Hepplewhite dining chairs in
one window, a splendid Queen Anne desk in the other.

Behind the desk a head bobbed and then was discreetly
withdrawn. When Forsythe stepped into the shop he saw
the young man had retreated to a seventeenth-century
commode and was wielding a feather duster. He was fop-
pishly dressed and his thin face was pitted with what looked
like acne scars. He was much too young for the man Forsythe was seeking.

"Mr. Ackerson is not attending to customers today, sir.
A sudden death, you see."

"I do. But I'm not a customer. Would you tell Mr. Ackerson, please, that Robert Forsythe would like to speak
to him."

After putting down the duster, the man scurried into
the dim recesses of the shop. Forsythe wandered over to
a display case and examined the contents. There were some
delightful Dresden ornaments and a beautiful shell snuff
box but his attention was caught by a jade Buddha. It was
a good piece but he decided not as good as the Buddha
given to him by Sir Amyas Dancer. That piece had been
the beginning of what now was a fairly extensive collection.

He looked up. The clerk was at his elbow. Rather breath-
ily he confided that Mr. Ackerson had consented to see
him. The clerk led the way, down an aisle, through a curtain of tinkling amber beads, opened a door, and bowed
in the barrister. Forsythe blinked. This room obviously
acted as living room, dining room, and study, and there

wasn't an antique in sight. The furnishings were modern and looked costly. The man seated in an angular, white leather chair looked expensive too.

Ackerson didn't rise but he waved a hand. "Don't look so shocked. Simply because I deal in antiques doesn't mean I have to live with them. Take a chair and help yourself to a drink if you'd like."

The moving hand waved toward a drink tray. Forsythe was about to refuse when he spotted a label. Laphroaig. This antiques dealer lived well indeed. After taking a generous tot of scotch, Forsythe selected another leather-covered chair. It proved to be comfortable. His host showed no signs of a sleepless night or overwhelming grief. Ackerson's skin was pink and healthy and his eyes were clear. His appetite wasn't suffering either. On a glass-topped table in front of him was a lavishly filled tray and a bottle of white wine. Ackerson was spreading pâté on a cracker.

"The condemned man is having a hearty meal," Ackerson said flippantly. "And if you're looking for an alibi for a murder that took place thirty years ago, you're out of luck."

"What's your alibi for last night?"

"I haven't a ghost of one. Jeff, he's my clerk, was having his day off, and so I shut up the shop about five-thirty. I spent the evening right here. Having dinner and working on books. I could easily have sneaked up to the home and poisoned the dog and done for Nanny."

"You're taking this rather lightly."

Ackerson poured more wine and took a sip. "That ass Taylor says I must answer your questions, but there's no way I'm spilling my guts to a complete stranger like you. How I feel about Nanny's death is my own business. Granted it was a horrible way for the poor creature to die. But Nanny was close to the hundred mark and her life expectancy wasn't long anyway."

"What about James Coralund?"

"Any grieving I did for Jamie was done years ago. Admittedly, having his bones found like that was a shock but . . ." He paused, to spread another cracker.

"You knew James Coralund was dead?"

"I *believed* he was dead. There's a difference." He fingered his bushy white sideburn and then stroked the end of a bulbous nose. "How is Hilary?"

"Inspector Taylor said that Dr. Falkner's nurse is staying with her."

"And no doubt Ben is dashing in and out. Wonderful chance for him to hover over Hilary."

The barrister decided this man did have some feelings. The small eyes were hot with anger and Forsythe remembered Miss Sanderson's conclusion about Ackerson. He *was* jealous of the doctor. Ackerson threw down a knife and pushed the tray away. "For years I've argued with Hilary. Told her there was no use in waiting for Jamie. If she'd only listened we might have been married and not wasted our lives like a couple of fools. Would you believe I proposed to that woman so many times I've lost count? I could have given Hilary the life she deserves. A nice house, clothes, luxury."

"You do seem prosperous. Inheritance or antiques?"

"Some of both. An uncle taught me the business and made me his heir. But I've done most of it by myself. Up until a few years ago I searched out antiques for collectors. Traveled a lot and made money hand over fist. I got tired of it and decided to give up that end of the business."

"From what I've seen of this town I shouldn't think there'd be much demands for antiques here."

Ackerson reached for the wine bottle. "Once you've made a reputation in this field there's no need to worry about local trade. The clientele comes to you from all over the country."

Putting his empty glass down, Forsythe looked at the bottle, but his host merely grinned and made no offer for further Laphroaig. The barrister settled for his pipe, but as soon as he pulled it out Ackerson snapped, "No smoking around me! Harry Moore had the brass to light one of his stinking cigars in here and I threw him out on his ear."

"I can take a hint," Forsythe said dryly.

"Take another one and get on with it. Exactly what do you want to know?"

"About your relationship with James Coralund."

"Ancient history." Ackerson sipped wine and his brow wrinkled in thought. "Here goes. Edmund Coralund was a kind of collector too. But he collected suitable playmates for his only son. I was only five when I was picked, and even as a little kid I must have been pretty sharp. I knew it was a profitable arrangement from the beginning. As kids the perks were great. Birthday parties and Christmas festivities, good food and scads of toys to play with. For a boy from my background it was mind-boggling. Mother and I lived in two rooms behind her little notion shop with the bathroom in the backyard. If I'd had a father around it might have been different, but Mother came here from somewhere in the north when I was a babe in arms and there never was a Mr. Ackerson in evidence. I used to ask my mother about my father but gave it up after a time."

Forsythe raised a brow. "She wouldn't answer your questions?"

"On the contrary. She raved on about him. One part of her stories was always the same. He'd died shortly before I was born. From there on it depended on the novel she was reading. Sometimes my father was a sailor who'd gone down with his ship, sometimes he was killed in war, once he was an Arctic explorer and was frozen to death." Ackerson gave a barking laugh. "Mother lived in a never-never land."

"You mentioned an uncle."

"Mother's older brother. Also an Ackerson. Uncle Ned

was a garrulous chap but that's one subject he never opened his mouth about. I finally decided Mother had been involved with a married man and he'd bought her off with the money to open her shop." Ackerson fiddled with a chain on his wrist. It was fashioned of heavy gold links and supported a Krugerrand. "Back to Jamie. At the manor I managed to live off the fat of the land while I was growing up. All I had to do was be Jamie's chum and tug the old forelock occasionally to his father. Edmund was a ridiculous chap. Hearty and backslapping and macho. But he was lavish. I remember one of Jamie's parties when Edmund hired not only a magician but a troupe of clowns. Of the three of us I think old Edmund liked Harry Moore best. Have you met Harry yet?"

"Not as yet."

"You'll like him too. Everybody likes Harry Moore. Of course in his business it's an asset to be friendly and hearty. He's much like old Edmund Coralund. Like Edmund in another way too. Neither good men to cross. One hell of a lot of violence under that genial exterior. I bait Harry on occasion myself but never push it too far. He could break me over his knee and—"

"You said you'd thrown him out on his ear for lighting a cigar."

"I was speaking figuratively, Forsythe." Ackerson fondled his fleshy nose and stretched out his legs. His sandals were highly polished and looked like Gucci. "I never got to know Jamie's mother that well. Marion Coralund was one of those mewling, puking women and spent most of her time in her own quarters. Jamie's sister, Agnes, was a haughty bitch and ignored all of us but Jamie. The person who actually ran the house and looked after the kids was Nanny Balfour. I soon discovered Nanny was another person you didn't cross. Even Jamie knew better than that. Nanny adored the boy but she didn't spoil him. If his sister and mother had had half a chance the boy would have been spoiled rotten. And, in any disagreement, Edmund always took Nanny's side."

"Edmund Coralund didn't spoil his only son?"

"No way. I always felt he was disappointed in the boy. Jamie looked like his dad but in temperament they were direct opposites. Took after his mother, I guess. Marion was supposed to be artistic and spent most of her time painting on china and doing embroidery and that sort of rubbish. And Jamie's prime interests were in music and books." He glanced up. "This the sort of drivel you want?"

"The background's fairly clear now. Could you tell me about the day of the party?"

"The last birthday party. For Jamie, anyway. When I got the invitation from Agnes I was tempted to tear it up. I was with Uncle Ned in Edinburgh learning his business and I could tell there was good money in it. I decided to go to the party because I wanted to see Hilary. The wedding was coming up and I was still hoping something would happen to break it off and—"

"Something did," Forsythe told him.

Ackerson jerked forward. "You insinuating I did it?"

"Merely stating a fact."

"Watch how you state facts or you're out of here." Ackerson settled back. "I'll admit I was overjoyed when it looked like the bridegroom had gotten cold feet and taken off. For a time I thought I had a clear field with Hilary."

"The day of the party," the barrister reminded.

Ackerson glared at the younger man but continued. "It looked promising when I arrived. I was the last guest to get there, and dinner was about to be served. They were the glummest bunch I'd ever seen. It was more like a wake than a party, and Jamie was being beastly to Hilary. He made a big fuss about most of his presents. I'd brought him a cigarette case, gold and costly, but I'd got it wholesale. He emptied his ghastly black cigarettes out of his old case and filled the one I gave him. He draped the horrible tie Joanne Drew gave him over his tennis shirt and then he kissed her. What a shoddy thing! Painted with flowers and doodads. The last parcel he unwrapped was a watch from Hilary. He was wearing a cheap, nickel-plated watch with a leather band and he wouldn't take it off. Hilary tried to and he jerked his wrist away, said he'd save the new watch for good, and thanked her very coldly."

Ackerson picked up the last cracker from the tray and nibbled at it. "Things went from bad to worse and after a set of tennis Hilary stormed off. Jamie had gone into a hot embrace with Joanne again. Andy Parker looked like he'd swallowed a dose of hemlock, and I was hoping he'd deck Jamie. Andy was hot for little Joanne. Didn't blame him. She was a tasty morsel when she was a girl. Should see her now. The size of a blimp!

"Of all the people at that party I think I was the only one enjoying myself. I could hardly keep a straight face, and I was hoping that Hilary would see the light and throw that diamond ring in Jamie's face. But no such luck. Her not-so-charming prince decided to break the party up right after supper, and the male members of the Gang walked our hero down to his lush pavilion." Ackerson grimaced. "Didn't even bother asking us in for a nightcap."

Eyeing the bottle of Laphroaig, Forsythe nearly grimaced too. The antiques dealer certainly wasn't open-handed with drinks himself. He asked, "What did you do for the rest of the evening?"

"The only person left around was Harry. And I can't stand the fellow. Great at physical prowess and a vacuum up here." He tapped his bald head. "But it was too early to turn in so we had a few games of billiards. Of course, Harry won and I got pretty fed up. While we were playing Agnes stuck her head into the room and asked us if we would lock up for her. Harry said sure and when I'd had enough I went up to bed and left him to do it. I guess he was the last one up."

"Are you certain the letter Jamie left was actually written by him?"

"I'm no handwriting expert but . . . yes, I'd swear it was his writing. Jamie had a distinctive handwriting." Ackerson stretched and regarded the tips of his Gucci sandals. "For a while I figured I'd grabbed the gold ring. The marriage had been pushed by Edmund and Marion and Nanny Balfour and, although Hilary was all for it, I don't think Jamie was keen on the idea. To be frank, I've always thought Jamie might have had something going with Joanne Drew. She was working in London while Jamie and Lee lived there and, as I said, she was a pretty girl then. And the day of the party she was certainly throwing everything she had in Jamie's direction. I figured Jamie had cleared out to let things cool down and then he'd break off the engagement. And faithful old Sean would be around to console the jilted bride."

Forsythe shifted in the angular chair and the leather creaked. "Have you any idea who might have killed James Coralund?"

"Any number of ideas. Maybe he'd had an affair going with Joanne and decided to break it off and she bashed his head in. The woman scorned, you know. It could have been her ardent suitor, Andy Parker, who now is a man of God but then was simply a young fellow pea green with jealousy. It might have been Harry Moore or Lee Dorf. Both of them were nuts about Hilary—"

"That I can't see. If Jamie was leaving Hilary practically on the eve of the wedding—"

"Could be one of them was making damn sure he wouldn't come back to her."

The barrister raised an ironical brow. "That motive also applies to you, Mr. Ackerson."

"It does but I didn't touch a hair of the dear boy's head. You're wasting your time, you know. Finding Jamie's murderer is similiar to discovering the identity of Jack the Ripper."

"You seem very sure."

"It's a cold trail. Lots of motives and not a shred of proof."

"Nanny Balfour's trail is still warm."

"A fool can see that it's tied in with Jamie's murder. The old girl had gotten senile and was babbling away in her sleep. She could have tipped someone on who did finish Jamie off."

Forsythe's eyes narrowed. "How do you know about that?"

"Because anyone forced to visit Nanny knew about it. Up to a few months ago she had all her marbles and knew exactly what she was saying, but the last couple of times I was nagged into visiting her Nanny dozed off and muttered away about the past. One time she was having a set-to with Agnes. Giving her hell and telling Agnes she didn't care how she felt about her young cousin, Hilary and Jamie had to be married—"

"Had to?"

"That's what Nanny said. She was a pretty forceful woman." Ackerson said impatiently, "This is boring and futile. I've got a feeling you're going to fall flat on your face on this one. Won't do your wonderful sleuthing reputation any good. Might better take your secretary and trot back to London."

"Thanks for the advice, Mr. Ackerson. Now for some questions, and if you don't answer them for me you will for Inspector Taylor. Was the home kept locked in the evenings? If it was, who would have keys?"

Ackerson grinned. "Yes, to the first question. Any number of people, to the second. The home is always locked tight at eight and all the trustees as well as the staff have keys. And you have heard wax impressions can be made, haven't you? The master key hangs on the wall behind the desk at the home. That desk seldom has a person on attendance. Be simple to slip behind the desk and take an impression."

The barrister nodded. "This fixation the trustees seem to have for Miss Coralund—"

"Fixation? Not a bad term, but I'll give you a better one. Try addiction. There are a lot of addicts around. Some hooked on drugs, alcohol, even food." He looked pointedly at the stem of the pipe protruding from Forsythe's breast pocket. "As well as nicotine. Harry and Lee and I are all addicts for Hilary Coralund. Have been since we were kids. But I'm kicking the habit. As soon as Hilary is back to somewhere near normal I'm giving her one more shot at being Mrs. Sean Ackerson. If she turns me down I'm selling this shop and taking off for warmer climes."

An excellent idea, Forsythe thought. This man's absence could only improve the town. He said mildly, "Sandy tells me the young doctor might have the inside track with Miss Coralund."

"*Young* is the key word. Ben Falkner's still wet behind the ears. Good God! He's at least twenty years younger than Hilary."

"I haven't met the lady but I understand not only is she beautiful but she still looks like a girl. Sounds tempting even for a young man. And I've known marriages like that to work out—"

"That tears it!" After lunging from his chair, Ackerson wrenched the door open. "Jeff!" he bellowed. "Show this shyster playing detective the door! As for you, Forsythe, you show your face here again and I'll rearrange it for you. If Taylor wants any more questions answered he can ask them himself!"

The barrister slowly got to his feet and as he passed his irate host he said coldly, "Better have that handsome young doctor check that blood pressure or you may not live to enjoy those warmer climes."

Ackerson brandished a fist and the Krugerrand jingled against the heavy chain. He howled, "Out!"

Forsythe eyed the fist and smiled. "I really wouldn't, Mr. Ackerson."

Whatever was in that smile caused the fist to waver and then fall. Ackerson took a couple of steps back and Forsythe made an unhurried departure. The clerk stood well back, fingering the scars on his thin face, his mouth slightly agape.

On the way back to the inn the barrister found he wasn't as cool as he had let on. Inwardly he was at a slow boil, and he wondered why Ackerson's head hadn't been bashed in years before. As he reached the Fiddle and Bow he decided that the antiques dealer was his favorite candidate for murderer.

CHAPTER 11

Miss Sanderson, waiting in the parlor of Hilary's cottage, wasn't feeling terribly happy either. She glanced at her watch for the third time in minutes. Nearly twenty minutes had elapsed since Dr. Falkner's gaunt nurse had admitted her and deposited her in this room.

She stopped pacing and perched on the arm of a threadbare chair, trying to interest herself in the surroundings. It scarcely was a suitable background for the beauteous Hilary. The cottage was built of white clapboard and needed repainting badly. This parlor had the feel and look of a furnished house before the next lot of tenants moved in. The walls were washed with gray paint that might have been left over from that used at the Coralund Home, the two chairs that faced a small television screen had seen better days, the only picture on the wall was a copy of one she remembered vaguely from her short life in her father's vicarage. A terrified deer was facing a circle of mean, hungry-looking wolves, and she believed it was called "Stag at Bay." The only cheer in the room came from sunbeams spilling gaily through the one small window. Miss Sanderson had a hunch that Hilary Coralund couldn't possibly spend much time in here.

"Miss Sanderson," the nurse called from the doorway.

"Miss Coralund can see you now. Sorry for the delay but when you arrived she was napping. The medication prescribed by Dr. Falkner makes one drowsy."

"Perhaps I'd better wait until tomorrow to visit her."

"No, she's anxious to talk with you. It may cheer her up."

Hilary's bedroom was at the back of the cottage, was much more spacious than the parlor, and was a far cry from the front part of the place. The walls were washed in a soft rose, the chiffonier and dressing table were antiques any collector might covet, and the bed was a huge four-poster. Hilary was not in the bed but reclining on top of a satin spread, propped up by pillows. She was wearing an azure brocade robe with a mandarin collar and a beam of light caught her fair hair like a halo. She was pale, had dark smudges under her eyes, and was incredibly beautiful. She gave Miss Sanderson a tremulous smile. "Abigail, I'm so glad you came."

"If you'd rather be alone—"

"No, I've had quite enough of my own company. Emma, do you think we might have a drink?"

"*You* certainly can't," the nurse told her. "Not with the medicine you've been taking. It doesn't mix with alcohol. I'll make a pot of tea."

The nurse bustled out and Hilary turned her head toward her visitor. "Emma takes wonderful care of me but she's very strict. I see you've noticed the lace on my pillow slips. Nanny made it for my hope chest. The sheets are edged with it too." Hilary's lips quivered and she said quickly, "Don't be nervous that I'm going to start blubbering on your shoulder. I'm all cried out. Now I only feel . . . rather detached. As though all this is happening to someone else. I can't really believe Nanny is gone. She was a big part of my life, and my mind keeps going 'round and 'round. Why would anyone ever hurt Nanny?"

"There can be only one reason for that," Miss Sanderson told her.

"No! Nanny adored Jamie. If she'd had any suspicion that he was . . . that someone had . . . Nanny would have told us immediately. She would *never* have protected the person who killed Jamie."

"I agree, Hilary. But Nanny might not have realized that she did have a clue to the murder."

The other woman winced. "If only that grave could have been discovered years ago. All these years of waiting, of hoping Jamie would come back. And all this time he's been there, right under the lawn I walked over."

Hilary was staring at a photograph of Jamie Coralund perched on her bed table. Another picture of the young man was on the dressing table, still another on the top of the chiffonier. On the wall at the foot of the bed was the group shot taken by Nanny Balfour. Hilary whispered, "If only Agnes had had the rose garden replanted. I remember asking her a few weeks after Jamie left . . . after he disappeared . . . why she didn't have the gardeners put rose bushes in there. She seemed indifferent and she said she was going to have it raked over and grass seed put on."

Miss Sanderson gazed down at her knotted hands. Her knuckles were white from pressure. This was going to be even worse than she'd anticipated. She forced herself to relax. She said gently, "Hilary, I don't think putting bushes in would have made any difference. They wouldn't have uncovered the body. You see, the grave was dug quite deep."

Hilary drew her breath in sharply, but to Miss Sanderson's relief a soft tap sounded on the door and Ben Falkner stepped into the room. He jerked a nod at Miss Sanderson and went directly to the bed. Gathering up Hilary's hands as gently as though they might shatter in his own, he said, "You're looking some better, Hilary. Taking your medicine like a good girl?"

"Emma's seeing to that, Ben. I am feeling better and I'm thinking of getting up."

"Maybe tomorrow. For now you're staying right in bed."
He lifted his head. From somewhere at the front of the
house a telephone was ringing. "Damn thing's been going
steady, I suppose."

Hilary smiled faintly. "Any number of people have
phoned. Emma's handled all the calls. I haven't . . . I didn't
feel up to talking to them."

"The ruddy fools should know better." He stopped and
asked, "What is it, Emma?"

"Emergency, Doctor." Emma was carrying a navy-blue
cape. "We're both needed. It's Alfred Bowles. Drove his
car into the front of the Guild Hall. As usual he was dead
drunk."

The doctor tenderly relinquished Hilary's hands and
straightened. "Alfred has something to drink about. He
hasn't worked for a year and his wife is about to present
him with another baby. This will be the fifth."

"Drink doesn't help," the nurse said severely. "But we
really must go, Doctor."

Hilary pushed herself up on an elbow. "Don't worry
about me, Ben. I'll be fine."

"You are not staying here alone. Emma will be back as
soon as possible. In the meantime . . . ." He turned to Miss
Sanderson.

She took the hint. "I'd be glad to stay with Hilary."

"Good. See she eats some supper, and she's to have one
of these tablets every four hours. Emma?"

The nurse pushed back a starched cuff and consulted
her watch. "The next one to be taken in one hour and
twenty minutes. Precisely."

The doctor turned at the door and looked back at his
patient. A man in love, Miss Sanderson thought, looking
at Hilary with the same longing that Hilary's eyes showed
when she looked at her dead fiancé's picture. He followed
his nurse and Miss Sanderson heard the front door close.

She got to her feet and smoothed down her skirt. "I'd better get that tea Emma was mentioning."

"If you'd care for a drink there should be some in the kitchen. In the small cupboard over the stove."

In the kitchen the teakettle was merrily boiling away and a tray sat on the table. Miss Sanderson measured tea and poured water in the china pot, put out a dish of digestive biscuits, and checked the cupboard over the stove. She could use a good tot of whiskey. She found the liquor supplies worse than scant. All there was was a lone bottle of cheap white wine. She opened the fridge to see if there was any beer but found only a couple of bottles of Perrier. She shrugged, put a second cup on the tray, and retraced her steps. As she handed Hilary a cup she said, "Lovely china. It looks like the set that was used for Nanny Balfour."

"It is. Part of the same set. All the furniture in this room came from my bedroom at the manor. I was hoping Agnes would offer a few pieces from the manor drawing room, but she sold nearly everything. Nanny persuaded her to leave the pavilion as it was, and when Agnes said she was selling the china and silverware Nanny put her foot down. Insisted I have my share, and she kept the rest. Nanny did like nice things around her."

"I noticed that. She must have loved flowers."

"Particularly roses. Once in a while I'd send Nanny some. I couldn't do it often. Everything is so expensive. Uncle Edmund and Aunt Marion provided an annuity for me but, like the funds for the home, it's barely adequate now. I suppose many people on fixed incomes have the same trouble. I can't even afford to dress decently now."

Miss Sanderson squeezed lemon into her tea. "Your dressing gown is charming. I've been admiring it."

"It was a gift." Hilary fingered a sleeve. "Last Christmas from Sean. He gave me a wonderful Hermès scarf then too." She smiled. "Luxuries, but what I really needed was a pair of gloves and some decent shoes."

"Sean seems most prosperous. Surely he's offered to help you."

Hilary's smile widened. "Not Sean. I think he's trying to starve me out. Force me to marry him. He's wasting his time. I'll never do that."

"Have you never considered marrying?"

"*Never*. And I could never marry either Sean or Lee. We were all so close to Jamie. It wouldn't be right." Hilary's lavender eyes clung to Jamie's pictured features. "To understand, Abigail, you'd have to had known Jamie. He was wonderful! Charming and sweet-tempered and gentle."

Hard shoes to fill, Miss Sanderson thought. "I was speaking with Mr. and Mrs. Parker earlier today. They told me about the birthday party. Their description of Jamie that day hardly sounds sweet and gentle."

"I'd never seen Jamie like that before." Hilary's fine brows drew together. "He seemed deliberately antagonistic. As though he was trying to hurt me. And he succeeded. He knew how I felt about Joanne Drew and yet he kept fondling her, even kissing her. And then when he opened my gift . . ." Hilary set her cup down with a clatter. A faint color seeped into her face. "I'd tried so hard to please him. He had this cheap watch that Lee had given him years before and it looked simply dreadful on his wrist. I'd bought him a handsome gold watch with a gold band and had the case engraved. Jamie looked at it and said, 'Thank you, it's very nice' as though he was thanking a stranger. He hadn't even lifted it out of the box. I told him it was engraved and then he did lift it and he looked at the back of the case. I tried to take his old watch off and he wrenched his arm away. And Jamie made such a fuss over his other gifts. Even the gaudy tie that Joanne had given him."

"Strange behavior for a bridegroom."

"It was. After the set of tennis when Jamie was hugging Joanne, I simply couldn't stand any more. I ran up to my room and opened the wardrobe and stared at my wedding gown and wondered what was wrong with him. It was such a lovely gown. It had been Aunt Marion's but Nanny remade it, and she'd mended a veil that Jamie's grandmother had worn at her wedding.

"I flung myself across my bed and wept. Later Agnes came up and told me we had to prepare supper, and when I went down I hoped Jamie was in a better mood. He wasn't and as soon as he ate he jumped up, said a collective good night, and went down to the pavilion." Hilary gazed off into space, her expression echoing a long ago hurt. "That's one thing I've never been able to forget. Jamie didn't even kiss me good night."

Blimey, Miss Sanderson thought, if I had been Hilary I'd have been pegging everything in reach at charming Jamie. She glanced at the little ormulu clock on the bedtable and reached for the vial of tablets. After shaking one into the palm of the other woman's hand, she reached for a water glass. Hilary obediently washed the tablet down, and Miss Sanderson asked, "Did you consider following him down to the pavilion?"

"By that time I was angry as well as hurt. But I knew we had to make up and I did consider it for a moment but the boys—Sean and Harry and Lee—followed Jamie and I thought they'd be in the pavilion with him. So I helped Agnes clear away from supper and then I went up to my room. I thought of going over to the wing where Nanny was and talking to her, but she wasn't feeling well that day and I thought she'd be asleep. I cried myself to sleep."

Hilary paused and then said slowly, "I was up early the next morning. I knew Jamie and I had to make up so I went down to the kitchen and fixed a tray for him. He wasn't at the pavilion and his bed hadn't been slept in. I

looked in the wardrobe and one of his traveling cases and
some of his clothes were missing. Then I went to the living
room. It was much as it was when I showed you that room.
The letter was on the desk and—" She broke off. "Abigail,
would you like to see that letter?"

"Yes."

"It's in the bottom drawer of the dressing table. Right-
hand side. In the jewel case. Do be careful how you handle
it. It's very brittle."

The envelope, a heavy vellum, was yellowed with age.
Across it, in an elegant black script, Hilary's name was
written. Miss Sanderson carefully extracted a single sheet
and looked down at that distinctive script.

"My darling Hilary," James Coralund had written. "I
know I hurt and disturbed you today and for that I'm
sorry. You must know you're the only woman I could ever
marry and the reasons for my actions have been confusion
and uncertainty. I worry that we won't be happy together.
As you may sense my music is the most important thing
in my life and it must take precedence even over my feelings for you.

"I've received a great deal of advice, some of it unwanted
and unsolicited. I know both Sean and Harry would like
us to postpone our wedding but, knowing how much they
want you, I find this far from objective. But I've spoken
with Lee and his advice I trust. He cares deeply for both
of us and advises we proceed slowly. And I feel Lee may
be right.

"As you know, my mother and father should never have
married and I've seen enough of that wretched sort of
existence. I have no intention of entering into an unhappy
marriage myself. I've decided the best course for me is to
get away from everyone and everything, to go off on my
own and think this out. I shall be back to give you my
decision. I feel it won't take long so expect to see me again

in a month, or at most six weeks. Believe me, darling, this
is for the best. Jamie."

Ye gods, Miss Sanderson fumed, as she replaced the
letter in the envelope and tucked the envelope back into
the jewel case. This, then, was the reluctant bridegroom
Hilary had spent her life waiting for. She asked abruptly,
"It is Jamie's handwriting?"

"Of course." Hilary had been mistaken about being be-
yond tears. Her eyes were brimming. "You see? Jamie *did*
love me. He *was* coming back. But someone . . . someone
took him away from me. Forever."

"Do you have any idea who that someone could be?"

Hilary dabbed at her eyes and her bright head fell back
against lace-trimmed pillows. "I've thought and thought.
Abigail, it's impossible. We all loved him."

One person certainly hadn't, Miss Sanderson thought
grimly. She wondered how to question this women about
her movements the night of Nanny Balfour's death. I'd
better sidle up to it, she decided. After clearing her throat,
she said, "Nurse Daley mentioned you were up to see
Nanny the other night. When we were speaking on the
phone you didn't mention you were going to visit her."

Hilary blinked. "At the time we spoke I had no intention
of going to the home. I'd worried about Nanny all afternoon but by the time I got home I was exhausted. Then
Joanne Parker rang up and said she was driving one of
the ladies from the church guild up to see an old uncle
who's a patient and would I like to go along." She sighed.
"Now I'm so glad I did go. Nanny seemed brighter than
usual and she managed to stay awake all the time I was
there. She was telling me about your visit, how nice it was
to talk with you, and she was so pleased with her dinner.
Nanny loved chicken, you see. I made a mental note to ask
Mrs. Blecker if she could serve it more often but . . ." A
single tear rolled down Hilary's pale cheek.

Miss Sanderson was tempted to give it up but then she lifted her chin. She must find out where this woman had been that evening. "Were you able to stay with Nanny for long?"

Hilary shook her head. "Only for about half an hour. Joanne drove me back here and when I came into the hall the phone was ringing. It was Lee and he wanted to know if I'd made up my grocery list—he does my shopping for me—and I told him no. He said not to bother, he'd ring me up the next morning. By that time I was too tired to think of cooking so I had a sandwich and a glass of milk and crawled into bed. I planned to be up early the next morning. For flag day, you know . . ."

As her voice trailed forlornly away, Miss Sanderson thought, Ah yes, that next morning. By then Nanny was dead and the bones of Jamie Coralund were being exhumed. She got up and picked up the tray. "You'd better rest for a time, Hilary. If you need me, call. Later I'll rustle up some supper."

The sunlight had moved farther down on the bed and now Hilary's hands rested in a pool of golden light. The diamond in her engagement ring sparkled like a tiny piece of ice.

Miss Sanderson wandered into the bleak parlor, glanced at the stag at bay, and retreated to the kitchen. She checked the fridge, found eggs and some cheese, and decided on an omelet and a salad for supper. Taking out lettuce and a tomato, she glanced at the kitchen clock. She might better phone the Fiddle and Bow and leave a message for Robby. He might be uneasy about her.

Mrs. Moore replaced the receiver and glanced across the bar. Forsythe was hanging his Burberry on a peg near the door. "Another message for you," she called.

"Miss Sanderson says to tell you not to wait dinner for her. She's at Miss Coralund's cottage. That didn't take you very long."

"Mr. Ackerson and I had a short interview."

The barrister's voice was low and controlled but Mrs. Moore shot him a knowing look. She lowered her own voice. "Don't pay mind to Sean. He's got a sharp tongue."

More like a wire brush, Forsythe told her silently. Aloud he asked, "What's delaying Sandy?"

"Emma Colt—she's the doctor's nurse—had to go off on an emergency and Dr. Falkner didn't want Miss Coralund left alone. Miss Sanderson says she'll leave soon's Emma gets back. Don't know what happened—"

"I do." One of the lads who earlier had been playing darts slouched into the bar. "It's Alf Bowles. Rammed his car into the Guild Hall. What a mess! I helped haul Alf out and he smelled like he'd swallowed a keg of beer."

"How bad is he, Ken?" Mrs. Moore asked.

"Hard to tell. But he was conscious and swearing and raving he wouldn't let no one but Dr. Falkner lay a hand on him."

"Well, he certainly didn't get drunk here." Mrs. Moore sniffed. "No way I'd serve that much to anyone."

A red-faced man at the end of the bar called, "Alf ain't got money for bar tabs now, Mrs. Moore. Hear he brews his own beer in a shed back of his house. Poor devil has nothing but trouble. Laid off from the mill and his wife expecting again. All them kids and Alf is dead broke."

"Well," Mrs. Moore said tolerantly, "he has had a run of bad luck." She drew a pint and shoved it over to Ken.

Tugging down his T-shirt, Ken snickered. "Can't see any connection between five kids and luck. Sounds more like Alf was doing too much—"

"And that'll be enough out of you, Ken Yates!" She turned her attention on Forsythe. "Anything you fancy, sir?"

His eyes roved along the row of bottles behind the counter. "By any chance do you have Laphroaig?"

"Sorry. No call for whiskey that costs that much. All we have is bar whiskey—oh, my Harry keeps some good stuff in his office. He came down awhile ago and he's in there now. I've got to get some food into him. Tell you what. If you like I'll bring your meal in there too."

Forsythe decided to accept the offer. It was a chance to kill two birds with one stone. He found Harry in his cozy office, huddled beside a roaring fire, his big head supported in two hands. The innkeeper lifted that head as though it weighed a ton. "Mr. Forsythe, is it? Sally said you wanted to talk to me."

"Only if you feel up to it. Hangover?"

"King size." The older man groaned. "Worst I ever had. Should have known better. Mind pouring your own drink? Don't think I could bear to."

"Mrs. Moore said you might have whiskey, Mr. Moore—"

"Harry. Don't like that mister stuff. Bottles are on top of that chest. Help yourself and bring the bottle over where it'll be handy."

Forsythe investigated Harry's supplies and selected a bottle of Glenlivet. He carried the bottle and a glass to a chair opposite his host. As the barrister poured, Harry Moore turned his head away. Forsythe grinned. "Is Glenlivet the name of the dog who bit you?"

"Wish it had been. Might not feel so hellish. But like a fool I started on gin and ended up on rum. And they didn't bite, they mangled. But enough of me, Mr. Forsythe—"

"If you're Harry, I'm Robert."

"Fair enough." The innkeeper gave the other man a doubtful look. "Figured you'd be older, around Abigail's age. But I guess age has nothing to do with brains, and I've heard a lot about you. Tell you one thing, I was glad to hear you were here and going to help get this sorted out. Yesterday . . . I couldn't believe what's happened. Now all I want to do is get my hands on the bastard who killed Nanny—"

"She probably died in her sleep," Forsythe comforted. "Didn't know what was happening."

"*I* know. Robert, she was so *tiny*. A little mite of a lady I could lift with one hand. And someone sneaked into her room and the son of a bitch—"

"Harry! That's enough of that." Mrs. Moore, balancing a loaded tray, stepped into the room. "You stop that cursing. And you eat every scrap on this plate. Mr. Forsythe, you make him mind!"

Forsythe chuckled. Harry Moore might be an old man, but he doubted he could make him do anything. The innkeeper was about two inches taller and about fifty pounds heavier. And that weight looked like muscle.

Harry's bloodshot eyes peered sheepishly up at his wife and he said meekly, "I'll eat, Sally. I swear it."

She patted his head and bustled out. Forsythe spread dishes on a low table and the two men proceeded to demolish the contents. True to his word, Harry ate every scrap, and when he pushed his plate away he looked somewhat better. "Down to business. Tell me how I can help."

"I have most of the details on the party, Harry. Ackerson told me you were probably the last one up that night."

"I was. Agnes had asked me to lock up, and after Sean ducked out and went to bed I wandered around checking the doors and banking the fire in the drawing room. Yesterday I went over and over it again. Can't think of one thing that points to Jamie's killer." Harry ran his fingers through the mop of salt-and-pepper hair. "When I found he'd gone missing during the night I wondered how he'd left the estate. I decided it must have been by car, so I ran out and checked the old stable that had been converted into a garage after Edmund Coralund died. Great man Edmund was for horses and he had a nice lot when he was alive. But Jamie's Mercedes was right beside Agnes's Bentley, and the only other vehicles that were there was the van my dad had lent me and Sean's uncle's sedan."

"Did you tell the others that?"

"Ran back to the house and did just that. Agnes said Jamie had probably walked into town and taken a bus or train. Seemed queer to me. I couldn't see Jamie lugging a suitcase that distance when he had a car right there."

Forsythe poured coffee, handed the other man a cup, and spilled a little Glenlivet into his. "We'd better go farther back. To when you were children. How did you get along with Jamie's father?"

"Like a house afire. Outside of my dad, he was the best thing that ever happened to me. Edmund really liked kids and he did so much for them—"

"Parties with magicians and clowns?"

Harry smiled. "Any kid is going to like that, but he did a helluva lot more. Remember the time Amos Dorf beat up on poor Lee. Lee's mom had just died and Jamie and me sneaked out to his house to see how he was. His father was out at the barn—we were all scared stiff of that man —and we looked in the window of Lee's bedroom. He was sprawled out on the floor, his face covered with blood. We figured he was dead and hightailed it off for help. As luck would have it Edmund Coralund was exercising one of his horses and we met him down the road a piece. When we told him Edmund whipped up that horse and galloped to the Dorf place. Jamie and I ran along behind and we got to the barnyard in time to see him doing a job on Amos Dorf with his riding crop. Edmund really lit into that bastard. Had Dorf blubbering and told him if he ever used his fists on Lee again he'd kill him. Meant it too. Edmund was a grand man!"

"Ackerson doesn't share your views."

Harry snorted. "All Sean wanted from Edmund was . . . well, everything he could get. Don't get the idea I'm talking behind Sean's back. I've told him the same thing to his face. He was always sucking up to Jamie's dad trying to get what he called 'the perks.' But Edmund saw right through him and Sean got what the rest of us did, no more and no less.

"Edmund and I got along fine. He used to say he wished Jamie was like me. Interested in sports, you see. For a time he tried to force Jamie to play soccer and learn to ride, but Jamie broke his leg in a soccer game and fell off a horse and cracked his wrist. Edmund was disgusted about the riding lesson. Said he wouldn't have minded the boy taking a tumble at a hurdle but Jamie had fallen off that horse like a bag of oats when it was standing still." Harry laughed. "That was when Edmund asked me what to do about Jamie and sports. I was only about twelve at the time and really puffed up being asked man-to-man."

"What did you tell Edmund?"

"To stop trying to force the lad. So Edmund eased off and sure enough by the time Jamie was fifteen he was a good tennis player and pretty fair at golf. Jamie just didn't care for rough sports."

Harry was lighting a cigar and his companion pulled out his pipe and began to load it. "Lee Dorf seems to resent his benefactor."

"Benefactor is the right word. Edmund was good to Lee. Even left Lee some money in his will. That sure had Sean hot under the collar. As I tried to tell him, Edmund wanted to make sure Lee had enough to get started as a writer. Sean was doing pretty good with his uncle and I was making out well with football. Lee was the one who really needed help." The innkeeper made a gesture with his cigar and ash spilled down his shirt. "I'd have thought Lee would be grateful."

"He never showed how he felt about Jamie's father?"

"Lee never shows much of anything. Keeps his feelings pretty bottled up. I've known him since we were toddlers, and all I really can say about him is he took Jamie's disappearance hard and adores Hilary. Of course, he was closer to Jamie than Sean and I were. Both of them kind of artists."

Leaning forward, Harry refilled his cup. "When we were all kids we were close but as we got older the Gang drifted apart. As soon as I left school I got involved with a football team, and we traveled all over the place. Mom wasn't for it, wanted me to stay home and learn the business, but my dad took my side and away I went. Dad never praised me to my face, afraid of making me conceited, I guess. But Maggie used to tell me every time my team won a game Dad would set up drinks on the house. Maggie was a great girl for a joke and said if we didn't start losing we'd put the inn out of business."

"When did Ackerson leave town?"

Harry's brow wrinkled in thought. "About the same time I did. His mother died and an uncle offered to take him in so Sean headed to Edinburgh. Jamie and Lee were at the manor for a few more years. They didn't go to London until after Edmund died. Edmund had been trying to interest Jamie in running the mill with about the same luck he'd had in teaching him to ride. Jamie just didn't take to it. As soon as Edmund was buried, Jamie put the mill into the hands of a manager and left town."

"And Hilary?"

"She stayed on at the manor with Marion and Agnes and Nanny. Marion was always in poor health and we all expected her to pass on long before her husband. But she outlived Edmund by about four years."

"Did you see much of Jamie after he left town?"

"I only saw him a few times. Once at his father's funeral, once at his mother's. But when I came back to town I'd go up to the manor to see Nanny and Hilary. They'd give me news about Jamie and Lee. Reading between the lines, I gathered Jamie wasn't paying much attention to Hilary and

I must admit I kind of hoped their engagement had pe-
tered out. But soon after Marion Coralund's funeral my
mom wrote and said Hilary and Jamie were formally engaged and he'd given her a ring. That's when I started
going steady with Sally. In May Hilary wrote and said their
wedding date was set for the twenty-first of June and
would I come back to town for Jamie's birthday party and
stay over for the wedding. It was to be a quiet affair because
of Marion's recent death. Lee Dorf was to be Jamie's best
man."

Forsythe rose and stood in front of the mantel. He took
a good look at the group photograph. Harry Moore had
been a husky young man and Agnes Coralund, despite her
smile, looked rather stern. He stared at Hilary Coralund's
glowing young face and then turned to look at the recent
photograph of her. Sandy had been right. This woman
hadn't changed. What was it Sandy had said? Ah, yes,
Hilary was frozen in time. There wasn't a sign of a wrinkle,
no sag along the jawline, in Hilary's lovely face. He admitted Inspector Taylor had been right too. Hilary's beauty
was similar to Grace Kelly's when she had been a young
actress. Princess Hilary, he thought sadly, and Prince Jamie. All their friends had aged but they . . . Jamie would
always, in the memories of their friends, be a handsome
young man, and Hilary was still a beautiful girl. He sighed
and asked, "Harry, have you any idea why Jamie was acting
so strangely toward his fiancée at that party?"

The innkeeper shrugged an enormous shoulder. "Guess
Jamie just felt like being nasty. Most of the time he was
easygoing but he could be ornery. Sometimes I wonder
what kind of a life he'd have given Hilary if they had been
married. But you can't blame Jamie. Nanny did her best
not to spoil him, but his mother and sister doted on him
and so did Hilary. Enough to make anyone selfish." He
looked appealingly at the younger man. "Can this sort of
stuff really help you?"

"I don't know," Forsythe said honestly. "But all we can do is keep on sifting, hoping someone will say something or *not* say something that will give us a clue."

"Do you think you and Abigail are making any progress at all?"

It was the barrister's turn to shrug. "I wish I could say yes but at this point we're simply feeling our way. Do you have any suspicion?"

"That's what I spent yesterday trying to work out. Take Sean and Lee and me. Sure, we all wanted Hilary and were hoping somehow Jamie would give her up but . . . Hell! No way we'd *kill* to get him out of the way. There was Andy Parker. He wanted Joanne as much as we wanted Hilary, but I can't see him killing Jamie. It was pretty clear Jamie was only flirting with Joanne. And there's no one else. Neither Agnes nor Nanny would hurt Jamie."

Forsythe stroked his chin. "I think we have to consider Nanny Balfour's death as the focal point."

"I've tried to work that in too. Look, Jamie had his head bashed in the pavilion—"

"Why the pavilion?"

"Common sense. It was a cool night and anyone who wanted to talk to Jamie would have had to go down to the pavilion. Jamie sure as hell wouldn't have hung around outside in the cold. So, after Jamie was dead the killer would have to lug his body from the pavilion to where the earth was turned up around the sundial. Nanny's bedroom window overlooked that area. Maybe she saw Jamie being buried—"

"Two questions, Harry. Was there enough light, say a full moon, for Nanny to see the burial? Two, if she had, would she have stayed in her room and not said a word about it?"

"There was no moon that night. It was black as hell. But the killer could have had some kind of light—say a flashlight." Harry shook a baffled head. "If Nanny had seen anything suspicious she'd have raised the roof. Had all of us up and out there."

"Unless—" Forsythe hesitated and then said, "unless the killer was a person Nanny would have protected. Another child she'd raised. Perhaps Hilary."

Harry's wide face flooded with angry color. "What a stupid thing to suggest! You're supposed to be a detective. Tell me this—what was Hilary's reason?"

"A number of reasons. Jealousy of Joanne Drew, for one. Perhaps if Hilary had found that Jamie was jilting her, she could have lost her head and killed him. Harry, we must explore all possibilities."

"I suppose so," the other man muttered. "But you're on the wrong track. Nanny raised Hilary, yes. But her favorite was Jamie. As my mom used to say, for Nanny the sun rose and set on her boy. Nanny Balfour would have turned Hilary in as fast as anyone else."

"That's what I've gathered," Forsythe said softly. "It must be something else that made Nanny dangerous. Perhaps some tiny fact she knew that no one else was aware of. Something she wouldn't have mentioned when her mind was still clear." Forsythe glanced at his watch and jumped to his feet. "It's well after nine."

"So?"

"So I'm driving to Miss Coralund's house and checking on Sandy."

"Fond of that lass, aren't you? And I don't blame you. Abigail is a grand lady. But a moment, Robert. You get wind of who did for Nanny, you tell me. From there on I'll handle it."

For a moment the room was so quiet that all that could be heard was the ticking of the mantel clock and the hiss of coal burning on the grate. Then, in a rush, two dogs trotted into the office. The one in the lead, a border collie, sniffed at Harry's knee and then sprawled full length on the hearth rug. The small terrier pawed at his master's

ankle, and Harry bent and lifted the dog to his knee. Forsythe noticed the gentleness of the innkeeper's huge hands
as he patted his dog. Like many powerful men, Harry
could show that gentleness to women, children, and animals. Harry lifted his head and their eyes met. Forsythe
repressed a shudder. This *was* the same type of man that
Edmund Coralund had been. He had a vivid picture of
what would happen to the person who had smothered
Nanny Balfour if this man was given a name. Those huge
hands, so gentle on the dog's head, would crush the killer
to death.

Forsythe shook his head. "Not the way you're thinking
of doing it. There'll be due process of law."

"Has that anything to do with justice?"

"If it didn't I wouldn't be a barrister."

Forsythe called a good night from the doorway, but
Harry was staring down at his hands.

CHAPTER 12

Forsythe was putting the key in the ignition of the Rover when he noticed headlights approaching. He got out, slammed the door, and in long strides walked toward the MG that was pulling up to the curb. Opening the window, Miss Sanderson peered out. He raised his voice, "It's about time!"

She rubbed an ear. "Lower your voice. I've had enough yelling to last a lifetime."

"Sorry." Putting a long arm around her shoulders, he gave her a quick hug. "As Harry Moore says, you're a grand lady and I shouldn't want to lose you. Yelling? Surely not Hilary?"

"Definitely not Hilary. I've never heard her raise her voice. Too ladylike. But Inspector Taylor came to her cottage awhile ago and she seemed better so I let him go in and talk to her. I was cooling my heels in her parlor, staring at a stag at bay, when Dr. Falkner and his faithful nurse Emma came galloping in. First the doctor sounded off at me and then stalked into Hilary's bedroom to have it out with Taylor. The gist of the conversation was that Taylor's a damn fool and Hilary is too ill to be grilled. Taylor started out reasoning and ended up shouting as loud as Falkner was. A great way to keep Hilary soothed."

"I'm beginning to find Miss Coralund intriguing. Perhaps I could interview her myself."

Miss Sanderson snorted. "To do that you'd have to get past her stalwart protector. Ben Falkner is head over heels about her."

"Even more intriguing. Exactly what is this lady like?"

"As you've heard, great to look at. Also charming and with an aura of fragile femininity. Under all that . . . I'd say quite an ordinary woman. Not terribly intelligent and still completely obsessed by the memory of her lost fiancé."

"Tremendously loyal."

"Tremendously nuts! You should read the letter Jamie left for her. All *I*'s. If *I* want, if *I* think it right."

"Would you repeat that letter?"

"Not now." Miss Sanderson shivered. "Right now I'm going to have a hot tub, a large smash of scotch, and about a dozen aspirin. Don't expect me on deck until about noon tomorrow."

"In that case"—Forsythe followed her into the inn—"I'll drop into the police station in the morning. I hope Taylor will have calmed down. Don't care for shouting myself."

The following morning found Forsythe in the inspector's office. Not only was Taylor calm, but his voice was normal. He brushed away his dispute with the doctor. "Ben's a bit of a hothead," Taylor told the barrister. "Blows off fast and cools down just as fast. Last evening he ended up apologizing and offered to let me continue questioning Miss Coralund. But I had all I needed."

"Needed?"

"Wrong term. All I got was more of the same details I'd gone through exhaustively with Mr. Ackerson and Harry Moore and Mr. Dorf. How did you make out?"

"A mass of the same details that you got. One thing I did neglect to ask Leroy Dorf was his movements the night of the dog poisoning and Nanny Balfour's death."

The inspector reached for a pile of file folders. "I can fill you in on that. Mr. Dorf stated that he worked later than usual in the library that evening. His assistant, Miss Hall, had been off with the flu and there was a number of tasks he had to do. He said he phoned Miss Coralund shortly before he left the library and they chatted about some shopping he was going to do for her. He reached his cottage around eight, cooked some supper, did a few household tasks, and watched television until midnight. That's it." Taylor looked up. "Ah, Larkin. That will hit the spot."

The young constable set the tea tray on the inspector's desk, glanced at the barrister with a certain amount of awe and a covert curiosity, and backed out of the room. Taylor handed Forsythe a steaming cup and reached for the creamer. "Not an alibi among the six of them. Mr. Ackerson was alone in his quarters behind his shop, Miss Coralund was alone in her cottage—"

"What about the vicar and his wife?"

"Much the same deal. Mrs. Parker was at the church until nearly midnight, arranging flowers and doing a few odd jobs. Her husband was at the vicarage working on a sermon and—but didn't your secretary fill you in on the Parkers? I understand she had lunch with them yesterday."

Forsythe stirred sugar into his cup. "We haven't had a chance to compare notes." He glanced at the man behind the desk. "You seem to hear everything that happens in this town."

"That's my job." Taylor grinned. "Had a visit from one of the suspects late yesterday afternoon. And this one was practically foaming at the mouth."

"Ackerson?"

"Yes, and he had a complaint to register. Told me if I wanted to ask questions to go ahead but he refuses to have anything further to do with you. I must admit I'm curious. Mr. Ackerson has a number of chips on his shoulder. Which one did you knock off?"

Forsythe was smiling widely. "All I did was mention that the young doctor seems to have the inside track with Hilary Coralund and that many marriages of disparate ages seem to work out well."

The inspector's grin widened and became a laugh. "That would do it! Ben Falkner's interest in Hilary nearly drives Mr. Ackerson wild." He sobered and said slowly, "I have come to one decision. I don't believe that Miss Coralund or Mrs. Parker had any connection with James Coralund's murder."

"On what do you base that decision?"

"Lack of physical ability. Neither of them would have been strong enough to have lugged the body to the rose plot and bury it."

After pulling out his tobacco pouch, Forsythe proceeded to load his pipe. "Have you seen the group photograph taken while the famous party was in progress?"

"Many times. Hmm ... I see your point. Both Hilary and Mrs. Parker looked quite athletic in that. And Jamie was tall but slight. Not a heavy man."

"Right. Also, a wheelbarrow could have been used to trundle the body in. Or either woman could have had an accomplice."

"I stand corrected." Taylor pushed an ashtray across the desk. "Superintendent Kepesake mentioned that your— what was it he called it? Ah, your forte is in spotting tiny details, items no one seems to notice. Kepesake said any number of times those tiny details have solved a case. Noticed any tiny detail?"

"If there is one in the information I got yesterday the penny hasn't dropped yet. Have you any further facts from the lab boys?"

"Some. The cash found in the grave does amount to one thousand pounds. The pathologist agrees with Dr. Falkner about the cause of death. A blow to the back of the head. We had the body of the Great Dane exhumed and it was definitely poisoned. Strychnine. Which doesn't help one iota. That poison is used in many garden and pesticide compounds. The vet says there were chunks of undigested beef in the animal's stomach. Our guess is that the beef was dipped in the poison and shoved through the broken pane in the shed window."

"Anything further on Nanny Balfour?"

"As I told you yesterday, her death was definitely caused by asphyxiation. Her room, the furniture, the bedside objects, were rich with a bounty of fingerprints. Staff, volunteer workers, all the trustees, the vicar, his wife . . . you name them and we have them. As for opportunity . . . just as hopeless. All that was needed was a key, and that would have been simple to procure. Access to the third floor is easy. Nip in the rear door, up the stairs to the old servants' quarters, into the nursery wing, and then into Nanny's room." Taylor threw up his hands. "I hate to sound depressed but I think we've got as much chance of solving this as of keeping snowballs firm in hell."

"Cheer up." Getting to his feet, Forsythe stretched. "The darkest hour is before the dawn."

Taylor lifted a hand and squinted along one finger as though aiming a gun. "You sound like one of the vicar's sermons. Rather unctuous."

Forsythe grinned and reached for his Burberry. "Ever notice clergymen and those in the legal profession have similarities? Using clichés, for instance?"

"Off for another interview?"

"Off to see if Sandy is out of bed yet. Perhaps after we have a chance to swap ideas something will emerge."

Miss Sanderson was not only out of bed but was sipping coffee and reading a newspaper in the bar of the inn. As her employer seated himself opposite, she folded the paper and raised a brow. "Confession time? Or, as Ted the TV personality would say, time to bang ideas?"

"Yes. But not here." He glanced around the room. Mrs. Moore and the barmaid were watching them and the dart players were paying more attention to their table than to their game. "All those pink little ears tuned in. Anything interesting in the local paper?"

"The usual tripe. Rehashing the crimes and a statement from the police. A number of leads and results expected momentarily."

Forsythe laughed. "That's not the way I heard it." He waited while his secretary drained her cup and then asked, "Have you still got Harry's keys. Yes? Good girl. We'll use Jamie's pavilion—"

"Could we call him something else? I'm getting a bit tired of that name."

"Such as?"

"How about the nerd?"

"What the devil is a nerd?"

"A kissing cousin to a wimp."

He laughed again. "Sounds as though you've been talking to Grace Penndragon again."

"I spent a couple of days with Grace in Dorset a few weeks ago. She'd added three new words to her COWW—"

"Cow?"

"Collection of witless words. After her brother-in-law's death I thought Grace would give that hobby up, but she claims it's hard to break."

"Sandy, I'm waiting for that third word."

"That's the best of the lot and I'm saving it for the proper moment. And before we bang ideas I'm going to have lunch."

"I spoke to Mrs. Moore about that last night. Lunch is waiting in a wicker basket in the back of the Rover. Glad to see your interest in food is more active."

Miss Sanderson's interest in food was active enough that they were heading for the Coralund Home in record time. She paused in the carpark and looked up at the stone manor. "Robby, my conscience is barking at me. I'd better take a moment and see how Maggie Murphy and her Poopsie are. Come along with me. You'll like Maggie."

Luncheon was over and they found Maggie in the sun room, her golden spaniel at her feet, working slowly and ineptly at a bright-blue garment that vaguely resembled a shroud. When she saw them her face brightened and she called, "There you are, dearie! Who's your young man?"

Miss Sanderson made introductions and Maggie called Forsythe "dearie" twice and "love" once. "I'm glad you came in," the old woman told Miss Sanderson. "I was just thinking of asking Nurse Daley if I could ring you up. Wanted to tell you how ashamed I am for saying those awful things to you about poisoning dogs. No fool like an old fool."

Forsythe stooped and patted the spaniel. "Where did you get the idea that Sandy was responsible for the Great Dane's death?"

"Josh kept ranting about those trustees and how they hate dogs. Not my Harry. Fine lad he is and loves pets. When Josh found out his Tiny was dead he yelled maybe that Sanderson woman had killed his dog. He had me so

upset when I saw her I just blurted it out. Drat!" She
fumbled with the shroud. "Never was a hand at knitting.
Dropped another stitch."

Forsythe had been eyeing the unwieldly garment with
fascination. "What are you making, Maggie?"

"A muffler for Josh." She held it out and regarded it
dubiously. "Do you think it's a mite too long?"

It was Miss Sanderson's opinion that Josh Pitts could use
it for an overcoat, but she said brightly, "Looks just fine.
How is he?"

"Still in the sickroom. I was up to sit with him for a
time this morning. His spirits are awfully low. Nurse
Daley says it's time he got up and around, but he don't
seem to want to get out of bed. Not like Josh at all. Say,
maybe you and your young man could drop in and cheer
him up, dearie."

"We'll go up now. Should I ask permission?"

"No need. Sickroom's at the head of the stairs. Josh will
sure be glad to see you."

As they mounted the stairs, Forsythe asked plaintively,
"Why would Josh be glad to see the woman he believes
poisoned his dog?"

"Perhaps to practice his cussing. Josh has swearing
down to a fine art. In his own words, he's full of 'piss and
vinegar.' "

The sickroom had four beds but only one was occupied.
Josh was flat on his back, his wrinkled face turned up to
the ceiling. He showed no interest in cursing and less in
his visitors. Miss Sanderson regarded him with concern
and decided on a frontal attack. "Maggie Murphy tells me
you think I killed Tiny."

"Guess it wasn't you. Don't know who could have done
it. Tiny wouldn't have hurt no one. Gentlest dog you
ever seen. Used to sleep beside my bed, and at night
I'd put out a hand and he'd lick it. Feel kinda lost without
him."

The poor lonely old devil, Forsythe thought. "Mr. Pitts, we're trying to find who did poison your dog. We suspect the same person was responsible for Nanny Balfour's death."

"Heard someone did her in." Josh's eyes left the ceiling and flickered toward the barrister. "Not pretending to mourn her. Hardly knew the woman. Awful thing to admit, but I feel worse about Tiny."

"That's only natural," Miss Sanderson said soothingly. "Tiny was your constant companion."

His eyes closed and when they opened he again stared listlessly at the ceiling. Across the width of the bed, Miss Sanderson's own eyes sought the barrister with an open appeal. This, Forsythe thought, was not the man who had reduced an entire TV crew to quivering wrecks. This was a man who was giving up. He spoke sharply. "Are you going to stay in bed and do nothing about your dog?"

"I'm old and useless."

"You still have your eyes and your ears and your mind. You could help us."

"How?"

How indeed? Forsythe wondered. Miss Sanderson took over. "Your memory must go way back. You must have known the trustees when they were young."

Josh's rheumy eyes moved in her direction. "Didn't know Miss Coralund or Mr. Ackerson at all. Seen Harry around the inn some. But I did know Lee Dorf. My wife and me had a little farm down the road from the Dorf place. The Brewster place was in between us. Amy Brewster was young Lee's mum." A trace of animation showed on Josh's face and he struggled up on his pillows. Miss Sanderson tried to help and he fended her off. "Still can sit up by myself. Amy was a pretty girl and a lively one. Had my eye on her a spell myself 'fore I got married. Amos Dorf got her in the family way and Lee was born only a few months after they run away and got married. The ladies of the town were sure hard on Amy. Never let her forget it. Times were different then and people frowned on that sort of thing."

He gave Forsythe a twisted grin. "Saw a television show awhile back where some actress was *bragging* about having two kiddies and them not having a legal father. Wasn't like that when Lee Dorf was born. Amy was—what's the word?"

"Ostracized?" Forsythe offered.

"Nothing to do with an ostrich but Amy was sure shunned. Funny, a lot of those women turning their noses up were no better'n they should be. Just didn't get caught at it. Take *Mrs.* Ackerson. Never a sign of a mister and nobody took on about Sean. Then there was Junie Moore. Her son was born about seven months after Junie and Sam Moore was married. They claimed Harry was premat-ure and Junie had a fall what brought him on." Josh smiled again, and this was the devilish grin Miss Sanderson had noticed in the sun room. "Remember my wife saying after she seen the baby if Harry had been any more mature he'd been wearing knickers. But those women give Amy a hard time as though they was pure as the Virgin Mary."

Josh paused for breath and Miss Sanderson rewarded her employer with a beaming smile. This brand of medicine seemed to be working. Plumbing the depths of Josh's memory was futile for them, but it was breaking through his apathy. She persevered. "I've heard Amos Dorf was hard on his wife and son."

"Hard? That bastard was a crazy, drink-soaked—just thinking of Dorf gets me riled up. He had people scared shitless and I was one of them. Powerful brute and half out of his mind. Once he beat up poor Amy real bad and

I went over to try and reason with him. He was in the barnyard, and when I started to talk he told me to wait a minute and he went into the barn. He came out holding this big black handgun and pointed it right at my belly button. Told me he'd taken it off a German officer in the war and if I ever pushed my nose in his affairs again he'd blow me in two. I'm shamed to admit it, but that was the last time I did."

"Edmund Coralund knew how to handle him," Forsythe said.

"Beat the living shit out of him! Edmund was a real man's man. Waded in on Amos and whipped him. That was the last time Amos used his bleeding fists on young Lee."

"What did you think of Edmund's son?" Miss Sanderson asked.

"Young Jamie? Hardly knew the boy. His dad sometimes brought him down to the mill—I worked there for a spell—and the kid acted like he was scairt of getting dirty. Seemed like a sissy."

"A genuine nerd," Miss Sanderson agreed.

"What's that mean?"

"A sissy."

"That's what I said." Josh looked from one visitor to the other. "This going to help you find who did for Tiny?"

"It may," Forsythe said cautiously.

Miss Sanderson was more positive. She used one of Harry Moore's expressions. "Better bet your boots it will, Mr. Pitts."

"You folks can call me Josh. Any other way I can help out?"

Forsythe stroked his chin. "Josh, you must keep your eyes and ears open. If you see or hear anything odd, ring us up. We're at the Fiddle and Bow."

Josh nodded. "Guess I'd better get up and around. Mind moving my canes over?"

Miss Sanderson picked up the canes. "Hadn't you better ring for an aide or orderly?"

"Time I need one of those young twerps to pull my pants on I'll lay down and die." He winked a bright eye. "I'll be in touch, folks."

As they left the room Josh Pitts was throwing back the blanket and dangling his legs over the side of the bed. He was wearing a nightshirt and his legs looked like twisted sticks. Miss Sanderson said anxiously, "Robby, do you think we should send up an aide?"

"You heard the man. Josh will manage. I should also imagine the phone at the inn may be ringing off the wall with salty messages from your friend."

"At least he'll be moving around and cussing again. You helped enormously. You know, for a barrister, you're not a bad chap."

"All barristers have hearts of gold."

"The rumor is that the gold is in their wallets." She added, "I'm starving."

He took her arm. "On to the pavilion."

Once in the living room of the pavilion, Miss Sanderson proved her appetite was back to normal. Forsythe unpacked the wicker basket, and not only did she eat her share of soup and sandwiches but part of his. Scraping up the last morsel of gooseberry tart, she leaned back and contentedly rubbed her stomach. "I take back what I said about the Fiddle's cuisine."

Forsythe gathered up Thermos jugs, mugs, scraps of plastic wrapping. "Shall we begin?"

She stretched. "You talk and I'll listen."

"I haven't your memory so I jotted notes on my conversations with Ackerson, Dorf, and Harry Moore. Much of this is repetitive. Their recollections of the birthday party tally, so I won't go into those details. You've probably had enough of that anyway."

"*Ad nauseam*. Robby, the vicar and his Joannie even recalled the menu for the cold buffet supper."

Flipping open his notebook, Forsythe sketched out the remainder of his conversations with the three trustees and the inspector. Then it was his secretary's turn. She reported in full. When she had finished she added, "My impression of Mrs. Parker is that she still is rather proud of Jamie's interest in her. And her husband is still violently jealous of that interest. Other than that . . . she is a jolly person and runs a cheerful if untidy house. Andrew is rather oily but loves his wife dearly." She flipped a hand. "That's the lot."

"Nothing much we didn't know, Sandy."

She was smiling. "I rather liked that word Lee Dorf used. Harlots. I didn't think people used terms like that any more."

"Any conclusions?"

"I think I would have liked Edmund Coralund. He may have been a womanizer and hell-raiser but he was colorful. I can't say the same about his son."

"You've taken an irrational dislike to a man you never knew. Sandy, that isn't like you."

"Blimey! James Hareford Coralund was a self-centered, egotistical pup."

"He was the one responsible for setting up this home for aged, indigent people. You have to give him that."

"I'll give him nothing. His *sister* was the one who did that."

"Agnes Coralund was only following her brother's wishes."

Miss Sanderson's brow furrowed in thought. "Can we be certain it *was* his wish? If he had lived he might have changed his mind. It also occurs to me that Jamie could have been trying to get rid of everything binding him to this town. If he was serious about the home, that would include the manor and the mill. Perhaps, judging by his treatment of Hilary, also his fiancée."

Forsythe leaned forward. "You don't feel he would have returned to Hilary and gone through with the wedding?"

"Not a chance. I quoted his farewell letter to you. Robby, it was *cold*. Granted, he tarted it up with a couple of darlings, but James Coralund was cutting free from his fiancée. I have the feeling that all that day he deliberately goaded her, trying to force her to call off the wedding. But Hilary, poor dope, was only too eager to forgive and make it up. She's a thoroughgoing masochist." Miss Sanderson paused and then said abruptly, "Which leads me to another thought. Something that occurred to me when you were recounting your conversation with Inspector Taylor."

"Connected with Hilary?"

"Yes. You said she was physically able to kill Jamie and could have buried his body. Robby, I don't believe she's mentally capable of acting the part of bereaved fiancée all these years. Doing her best to keep the memory of Jamie Coralund green and flourishing—"

"You're eliminating Hilary from our list of suspects?"

"Stop interrupting, Robby. The first time I met her, at the Guild Hall, she said it was possible that Jamie was suffering from amnesia. Suppose that she did kill her fiancé in a fit of jealous rage? With a shock like that isn't it conceivable that Hilary blanked the whole business out of her mind? That she—"

"Doesn't know she did kill him?" Forsythe interrupted again.

"Precisely."

He glanced around the room, at the sheet music scattered over the top of the piano, the slippers nestled near his chair. "I can blow that theory to pieces, Sandy. If this is the truth why did she panic when the Great Dane started digging up the grave? Why did she smother Nanny Balfour?"

"Simple." Miss Sanderson gave him a beaming smile. "Because she didn't. You were the one who said she might have had a confederate. Remember, there were three young men here at the time of the murder, and all of them admit they were in love with Hilary. Maybe one of them buried Jamie's body to protect her. Maybe one of them continued to protect her by killing the dog and the old nurse."

Forsythe's long fingers were drumming rapidly against his knee. "Fanciful . . . but possible. Sean Ackerson, Lee Dorf, Harry Moore. I'd put my money on the accomplice being Ackerson."

"And I take irrational dislikes!"

"This is eminently rational, Sandy."

"In a pig's eye! I've seen Sean several times. I'll admit he can be a bit caustic but he's certainly been decent to me."

"Because he wanted your help to ban dogs from the home."

"Because I didn't deliberately bait him about the doctor's interest in Hilary Coralund. Admit it, Robby, *you* did. The other day you were psychoanalyzing my feelings about Aggie. Now, it's my turn. I can tell you why you don't like Ackerson. It isn't because he called you a shyster and threw you out of his shop. It's because he didn't offer you another drink of his scotch—"

"That's even more fanciful than your theory about amnesia." Forsythe flushed hotly. "I'm trained to be objective—"

"Your turn to listen. We'll try the word-association test. Right? The first word is Laphroaig."

"Easy. The Isle of Islay."

"Do you know what Laphroaig means in Gaelic?"

Forsythe relaxed and grinned. "Haven't the foggiest. All I know is that the whiskey is smooth and has a wonderful smoky taste."

"It means the 'beautiful hollow by the broad bay.' "

"If I didn't know better I'd swear you'd laced your coffee with the beautiful hollow by—"

"Back to word association. The Isle of Islay. Quick now."

"Jennifer Dorland and the week we spent on that island."

Miss Sanderson nodded her gray head. "A most romantic week walking by the sea and no doubt swallowing copious amounts of the famous scotch. How long is it since you've seen Jennifer?"

"As you well know, Dr. Freud, not since the end of that week. Jennifer's been in Los Angeles, New York, Rome, and Paris. As you also know she's a scriptwriter and has little time to spend in London."

His secretary spread both hands. "I present my case. You're missing the lady and when Sean Ackerson didn't offer another drink of the scotch that reminds you of her you subconsciously settled on the poor chap as murderer. And I don't blame you for missing Jennifer. I thoroughly approve of her. She's intelligent and talented and attractive. Jennifer also has a sense of humor. She'd make a perfect wife for you, Robby, and it's high time you were married—"

"Sandy."

Paying no attention, she rattled on. "Much as I hate to interfere, it's high time we had a talk. You're hopelessly old-fashioned and your sole objection to Jennifer is her career. Your idea of a wife is a demure little woman who will stay at home and tend the hearth and children. Come up to date. Many successful marriages now are between people who juggle separate careers and still manage to love and respect each other. You should propose to the girl."

Forsythe had settled back and was placidly lighting his pipe. He puffed out a cloud of smoke. "Sandy, you're trying to be a matchmaker and it won't work. Jennifer and I have discussed marriage and agreed that at this point it won't work either. I've no objection to a woman having a career, but to have a marriage it's necessary to see your wife or husband *once* in a while. Jennifer's work keeps her away from London about ten months a year. My work keeps me in London about ten months a year. We'd end up seeing each other for brief holidays and perhaps a weekend now and again. Great opportunity for a home and children. Now, shall we drop the subject? Right now we're trying to solve two brutal murders."

"So we are. We'll postpone this for another time. I've strayed from the subject. What were we—" She stopped abruptly and stared at the barrister. Then her eyes wandered past his shoulder and settled on the photographs on the piano. She lifted her hand and began to tap her front tooth with a thumbnail.

He jerked forward and watched her. Finally he murmured, "Sandy?"

"You just said the words, Robby. Marriage . . . *home* and children."

His eyes widened. Then he dropped his pipe into the ashtray and got up. He paced the length of the room. "Right," he said. He paused by the piano and gazed down at the two young faces. "Tall and slender and fair." Swinging around, he pointed at the desk. She nodded and Forsythe said softly, "That's the answer, then."

"Part of it," Miss Sanderson said crisply. "The rest—"

"Yes." He pulled a notebook from his pocket. After tearing out a sheet, he handed it to his secretary. "Do you have a pen? Very well, we'll both write it down. In full. Then we'll compare notes."

Their heads bent and they wrote. Miss Sanderson paused frequently to nibble at the end of her pen but the barrister wrote steadily. He was finished first and bent to pick up his pipe. After cramming more tobacco into the carved bowl, he lit it. Smoke was wreathing around his head when Miss Sanderson said, "That covers it. Pass your notebook over."

He did and in return received her sheet. They read as avidly as they had written. Then Miss Sanderson lifted her head and finally used the third word from Grace Penndragon's COWW collection.

"Awesome," she breathed.

CHAPTER 13

"Awesome," Forsythe echoed. "And impossible to prove. Not a shred of evidence that will stand up in court. If we take this to Inspector Taylor, he'll laugh us out of his office."

"We're right, Robby, I feel it in my bones. Everything dovetails. Where do we go from here?"

"We'll have to try for a confession."

"Blimey! A confession from a person who killed a helpless old woman and a harmless dog to cover up the first murder?"

"Have you another suggestion?"

"Bait. Dangle a hint that we know all. Try to force—"

"Another murder? Yours, this time? No way, Sandy, I'm not putting you in danger."

"Actually I was considering you as bait."

"I'm not putting me in danger either. I'm not a James Bond."

She was gnawing on a knuckle. Then she sprang to her feet and walked over to the mullioned windows at the front of the room. After pushing back a curtain, she stared over the hawthorn bushes at the towering bulk of the Coralund Home. While they'd talked clouds had drifted in, the sunlight had vanished, and it was as gray as twilight.

Lifting her eyes, she stared at the darkened nursery windows and the one that marked the room where Nanny Balfour had lived for over half a century. She could see the outlines of rose-covered curtains. As she stood there the first drops of rain spattered against the panes. Behind her, Forsythe switched on a table lamp. "All we can do is try for a confession," she muttered.

"I'm afraid that's it," he agreed. "In this room. We'll set the stage and bluff our way. I don't suppose there's a telephone here."

"No reason for one. The closest one I know of is in Nurse Daley's office."

"Use that . . . no. You'll have to go back to the inn anyway. Use one there."

"Why the inn?"

"Because you must steal that group photograph from the office. Then you ring up our candidate and say we're calling a meeting for the people who attended that party. Sandy, make it sound convincing. Better pick up some sandwiches and come back here."

"What time shall I say the meeting is to be held?"

"Eight. This evening."

She picked up her coat. "Steal a photo, make a call, pick up sandwiches. What will you be doing?"

"Cogitating."

"While you're cogitating try to figure out where that missing object is. If we could get our hands on it we might have a piece of evidence." She looked around. "Could it be here?"

"Not in this room. Yesterday I went through all the drawers in the desk and that chest looking for an extra glass."

Miss Sanderson dropped her coat over a chair. "You take the back bedroom. I'll take the other."

She stepped into the front bedroom and found it had once been used by Jamie Coralund. Military brushes and a picture of Hilary Coralund were on top of a bureau, underclothes still filled the drawers, suits and a couple of topcoats hung in the wardrobe. She was still searching when Forsythe joined her.

"Nothing at all in the back bedroom," he told her. "It must have been used as a guest room. I checked the medicine chest in the bathroom too. Any luck?"

She was going through the pockets of a suit. "Nothing but a couple of ticket stubs and mothballs." Reaching up, she ran a hand across the shelf. "A tennis racket and a package of golf balls. Damn!"

"It was a slim hope."

She shrugged and shut the wardrobe door. "Probably destroyed years ago."

"I'm not so sure, Sandy. You must remember this wasn't a murder inspired by hate. Love was involved and it could have been kept as a memento."

"Grisly." She shivered and moved closer to him. "This room is spooky too. The way all Jamie's possessions have been kept. You'd think he'd just stepped out of this room. By the way, I've had a thought. This is grisly too. Robby, three weapons have been used. A bludgeon, poison, a pillow."

He patted her arm. "You're considering our suspect may arrive armed with another weapon."

"It crossed my mind. While I'm at the inn do you think I'd better try to steal a revolver?"

"You know how I feel about firearms."

She looked up at him. "What do we do if I'm right?"

"We use reasoning, Sandy, sweet and gentle reasoning."

More than three hours later Miss Sanderson and Forsythe stood on the silky Persian rug in Jamie Coralund's living room, staring down the barrel of a black Luger. The barrister had managed to edge in front of his secretary, but she knew that not only was the weapon trembling but so was the hand that held it.

"All right, genius," she hissed. "Use that gentle reasoning."

Forsythe stepped a pace forward and the barrel dipped and then pointed at his stomach. "Don't be a fool," the barrister said firmly. "Inspector Taylor knows where Sandy and I are. And he knows who's with us. Violence isn't going to help. Put that gun down!"

The Luger wavered and then was reversed and handed, butt first, to the barrister. Miss Sanderson, who was shaking as badly as the hand that had held the gun, managed to keep her voice steady. "I'd say that was an open admission of guilt, Lee."

Lee Dorf stumbled over to a chair and sank on it. His face was the color of putty. "An open admission of fear. After what has been happening around here anyone would worry about a voice on a phone making an appointment in a lonely spot like this. That revolver belonged to my father. He used to brag he took it from a German officer and killed the man with it. I don't know if it's even loaded."

"Lee's fast on his mental feet," Miss Sanderson told the barrister.

"Extremely agile. But it won't wash, Dorf. When Sandy rang you up she identified herself, and you must have recognized her voice. When you arrived here you unlocked the door and crept in. You saw us before we knew you were in the house and yet you still threatened us with that Luger."

"It was only a voice on the phone. It could have been the murderer. And all I was doing was taking a look around before—"

"We're well aware of just who the murderer is." Forsythe carried the Luger to the desk and gingerly slid it into the top drawer. "You might as well drop the act."

"Hoping I'll say something to incriminate myself?" Dorf sneered. He glanced around the room. "I suppose you have a taping device set up or Inspector Taylor is lurking within earshot."

After pulling over a chair, Forsythe sat down opposite the older man. "I give you my word Taylor isn't here, and there's no tape machine."

Dorf's eyes narrowed and he scanned the other man's face. "I'm inclined to take your word. It would seem we can speak freely then. It sounds as though you suspect me of murdering not only Jamie but Nanny Balfour."

"We *know* you did, Dorf."

Dorf gave a mocking smile. "Ah, but can you *prove* it?"

Miss Sanderson said staunchly, "If we couldn't you wouldn't be here."

Dorf's eyes ranged around the room, lingering on the untidy pile of ledgers and old letters on the desk, flickering over the group photograph propped on the table at Forsythe's elbow. "This might be interesting. Tell me, what do you base this absurd accusation on?"

"Facts," Forsythe said flatly. "Fact one—you were James Coralund's half brother. Fact two—you were also involved in a homosexual relationship with him. Fact three—"

"My, what a mountain of facts. Or I should say conjecture? Don't bother trying to intimidate me with your courtroom manner. Granted you're impressive but, as you said a moment ago, it won't wash. That's a bunch of errant and possibly slanderous nonsense. But I do find it amusing. What do you base fact one on?"

"This afternoon Josh Pitts told us about your mother. Amy Brewster was pregnant with you when she married Amos Dorf."

"Good God, man! Half the women in this town were pregnant when they were married. Harry Moore's mother was and Sean has never known who his father was. Why pick on me?"

"Because of this." Forsythe pulled out a pen and placed the tip of it on the pictured face of a younger Lee Dorf. "Look at these features and then the faces of Hilary and James Coralund in that photo on the piano. Those fair good looks, the coloring, those distinctive features. They're a trademark in the Coralund family. The way you wear your hair nearly hides your brow but it's the same broad, beautifully shaped forehead all the Coralunds have. Look at your chin. Tapered exactly like Jamie's, Hilary's, Edmund's. If your nose hadn't been broken I have a feeling it would be delicate and high bridged." Forsythe moved the pen. "Now look at Sean Ackerson. A fleshy nose and tiny eyes and a heavy chin. As for Harry Moore—"

"Big, hulking, and dark," Dorf muttered. "Now you're going to claim that Edmund Coralund had another woods colt on the way and paid off Amos Dorf to marry my mother."

"Correct. Edmund's second wife, Marion, was pregnant with Jamie at the same time. No matter how Edmund felt about Amy Brewster he wasn't going to give up a legal child. And consider Edmund's treatment of you. Not only did he select you as a chum for Jamie but he kept an eye on your welfare. Edmund was the one who protected you from Amos Dorf, who brought you to the manor to educate and care for, who made provision in his will for you."

Dorf stretched lazily. "You'd have made a better fiction writer than I ever did, Forsythe. But tell on. Fact two?"

Miss Sanderson had been leaning on the back of Forsythe's chair. She straightened and gave the librarian a look of sheer revulsion. "If Hilary hadn't urged me to visit Nanny Balfour I doubt we'd have unearthed this. We know that, according to Harry Moore, you were close to Jamie in your childhood and stayed that way when you were young men. You remained at the manor with him until Edmund's death, you then went to London with him and shared a flat. But Nanny was the one who proved you were lovers."

Dorf made an applauding gesture. "Bravo! You're almost as good at this as Forsythe is. But then you've had a lot of practice, haven't you?"

"Almost as much as you've had acting a part," Miss Sanderson snapped. "While I was chatting with Nanny she dozed off and had a one-sided conversation with Jamie. She said two things that at that time meant nothing to me. Nanny was reliving her effort to convince Jamie that he must marry Hilary. She said, 'Jamie, you must have a home and children.' And then, 'The other can never give you those.' "

"I can explain that," Dorf said. "Jamie was once interested in Joanne Drew. After she came to London to work he squired her around and became involved in an affair with her. It's common knowledge that Joanne couldn't bear children and—"

"That occurred to us. But it was the way it was worded. Nanny definitely said *home* and *children*. Joanne was as capable of providing a home for James Coralund as she has for Andy Parker. But the clincher is this. Nanny then said, 'I don't care what you say, if your father knew he'd be rolling in the grave.' The descriptions we've had of Edmund Coralund all point up the fact he was a hell-raiser, macho, a man's man. Edmund would have been *delighted* that his son was having an affair with a woman. How would he have felt if it had been a *man?*"

"My word," Dorf drawled. "You two have really been piling up circumstantial evidence. Tell me, did Nanny say these damning things with any other witness present but you? Ah, I see by your expression you were the only one there. Anyway, Nanny was senile." He swung on Forsythe. "How would that stand up in court, barrister?"

"It wouldn't," Forsythe said bluntly. "But it did put us on the right track. Now we know what led up to that birthday party, what happened that night. Would you like to hear about it?"

"Don't stop now. I'm practically tingling with anticipation."

Forsythe steepled his fingers and gazed down at them. "I don't know when Jamie and you became intimate. Possibly after you came to live at the manor. No wonder you showed such disgust at Edmund's birthday present for you. Harlots! House of ill repute! But you did become lovers and went merrily off to London to continue that affair. Nanny either knew or strongly suspected what was going on, but she never would have betrayed her boy. She did put pressure on Agnes and Marion Coralund to marry Jamie off to Hilary.

"Jamie was desperate to break off the marriage he was being forced into and so the two of you made plans. At the party Jamie was to act boorishly toward his fiancée, hoping to enrage Hilary to the point that *she* would break it off. That didn't work but you had a backup plan. The money was all ready for Jamie to drop out of sight for a time. That evening he was to pack a few clothes, leave a letter for Hilary, and then leave. Probably in his Mercedes. After a cooling-off period Jamie would come back and tell his fiancée he couldn't go through with the marriage. He'd also break all ties with this town. He'd sell the mill, turn the manor into a nursing home, tuck Nanny away in it, and return to London to continue his life with you—"

"One moment. The money from my legacy was nearly exhausted. If Jamie was going to use the funds from the mill to endow the home, what were we to live on?"

"I don't imagine Jamie would have been impoverished," the barrister said dryly. "No doubt he had ample funds from his father's estate to keep you going. But to continue. Late that night, after Harry Moore retired, you came sneaking down here to the pavilion to say good-bye to your lover. By that time I think Jamie had packed, written the famous letter, and was preparing to leave. He'd also had time to do one other thing. Selling the mill was very much on his mind. So he burrowed in the desk, which once had been used by his father, to look at the records. While he was going through the drawers he found proof that Edmund Coralund was also *your* father and—"

"What proof?" Dorf asked.

"Probably a letter from Amy Brewster." Forsythe's hands fell into his lap and he stared at the other man. "Up to that point neither Jamie nor you had any idea of your blood relationship. Jamie had been willing to enter into a relationship with another man, but he couldn't stomach the fact that that man was his half brother. Incest repulsed him. When you arrived Jamie told you he was discarding you. And . . ." Forsythe's brows drew together. "I think he announced he was staying right here and going through with the wedding."

Miss Sanderson moved restlessly. "And you lost your temper and bashed the back of his head in. The act of a coward. The same cowardice that let you smother a ninety-seven-year-old woman. I've known many murderers, Lee Dorf, but you take top honors as the most despicable."

The contempt in her voice didn't appear to disturb Dorf. He merely smiled. A complacent smile. "Even if you're right, and I'm not saying you are, what can you do?"

"A great deal." Forsythe looked off into space and a grim smile tugged at the corners of his mouth. "The first case Sandy and I were involved in was the murder of a man who had died a quarter of a century before we were called in. Despite the time lag we *proved* who the murderer had been. We never give up and we won't give up on you. We also have a jumping-off place. You gave Jamie a watch. According to your friends it was a cheap, nickel-plated thing with a leather strap. The watch in the grave was the

gold one Hilary had given him. At the birthday dinner
Jamie refused to take your watch off his wrist. I don't think
he could afford to. Your watch was engraved with a touching and unmistakable love token. This one was from *you*.
So, we look for the watch."

"Good luck!" Dorf threw back his head and laughed.
"If I was the murderer I'd have destroyed that damning
evidence."

"I'm inclined to doubt that. You'd have considered it the
last link with your lover. It won't be difficult to get a search
warrant."

Dorf shrugged his shoulders. "Go right ahead. You can
tear my cottage apart and you won't find anything but a
few sticks of furniture and some clothes."

"I don't have your cottage in mind, Dorf. The first place
we'll look is in that locked drawer in your office at the
library. That's where you keep your copy of the group
photo. I have a hunch we may find something else. Perhaps
a letter to Edmund Coralund from your mother."

The older man no longer looked as confident. He
pushed back the lock of hair from his shapely brow and
fingered the jagged scar. Then he straightened and looked
from Forsythe to his secretary. "You're bluffing. Trying
to panic me. Suppose the watch and letter *are* there? All
that would prove is that Jamie was my half brother and
our feelings for each other were far from brotherly. I don't
think you can convict a man for his sexual preference or
a blood relationship."

Miss Sanderson looked desperately at her employer, but
Forsythe didn't spare her a glance. He was steadily re-
garding the other man. "Again, you're correct, Dorf," he
said tonelessly.

Forsythe got to his feet slowly, as though he'd suddenly
aged. He started pacing back and forth and then paused
beside the piano and looked down at the young faces in
the silver frame. "Did you know, Dorf, that I come from

a long line of barristers and judges? In some families certain professions seem to run, and Forsythes have always been drawn toward the legal profession. When I think of my grandfather, my father, a fragment from Psalms occurs to me. 'The sweet remembrance of the just/Shall flourish when he sleeps in dust.' "

"Touching," Dorf said mockingly. "But what—"

"I serve the cause of justice, Dorf, to seek justice for those who often can no longer seek it themselves. People like James Coralund and Nanny Balfour. Then I think of what Lord Mansfield once said during a famous trial. 'Let justice be done, though the heavens fall.' "

The barrister turned and his fine features looked as though they'd been carved from marble. "What I'm going to do will destroy every precept by which I live. I've never believed in vigilante justice no matter what the circumstances. But you are correct. I've been bluffing and there's no way to prove that you killed a young man and an aged woman. For the first time in my life I'm stepping away from all my beliefs—"

"Do stop!" Dorf was laughing. "You're going to turn me over to a lynch mob? In this little town? Come on, Forsythe!"

"I'm going to do something worse. I'm going to turn you over to Harry Moore." Dorf stopped laughing and sprang to his feet. Forsythe waved him back. "You know what he'll do, don't you? You can run and hide but Moore will find you—"

"He'd rip me apart!" Dorf crumpled to his chair. "He's exactly like Edmund Coralund."

Forsythe was white to the lips. "You have your choice. Harry Moore or the courts. Make it!"

The older man's bravado had vanished. His features were blanched and drawn and the weary eyes fluttered shut. "Then there is no choice . . . but hear me out. In most of the details you were right. That night when I came down here Jamie was sitting at that desk over there. He was drinking and the air was thick with cigarette fumes. The letter he'd written to Hilary was at his elbow but he was reading another letter, one that looked old. When I came in he swung around and looked at me as though he . . . as though he hated me. He handed me the letter. It was from my mother, and she was reproaching Edmund Coralund for forcing her into a marriage with a man like Amos Dorf. She knew Amos and she knew what a beast he was. She told Edmund that Amos would never treat her well and would take out his hate on her unborn child. She begged Edmund to at least look after his child. It was pathetic . . .

"I tried to reason with Jamie, telling him this made no difference to us, that all that mattered was our love. Jamie said his love had vanished, that he would never forget I was his brother. He said he never wanted to see me again. Then he tore off the watch I'd given him and threw it on the floor. He put Hilary's watch on his wrist. He told me he intended staying on and he would marry Hilary. Jamie said that was the only way he could seek his salvation."

Dorf's eyelids fluttered and he stared up at the shadowy ceiling. "His mind was made up and he couldn't be swayed. I tried one last time to embrace him and he struck me right here." He touched his shattered nose. "I went wild. It was as though Amos Dorf was beating me again. I struck Jamie repeatedly and he flew back and fell. Jamie sprawled on the floor and at first I thought he was just unconscious. Then I found he'd struck the back of his head on the corner of that hearth. He was dead. After I dug the grave in the rose garden I carried his body and then his suitcase out and I buried him. When I came back in here I saw the watch on the floor, my mother's letter on the desk. I should have destroyed them but . . . I couldn't. My mother . . . Jamie."

"You'll make a confession?"

"Yes." Dorf drew a deep breath. "You can get Taylor but . . . I've two conditions."

Forsythe's lips tightened. "No conditions."

"You won't object to these. They won't interrupt the course of that justice you serve." He fumbled in a pocket, pulled out a key ring, and worked one key loose. He handed it to the barrister. "After my confession is signed and witnessed I want you to destroy Jamie's watch and my mother's letter. You see, I'm going to give another motive for Jamie's death."

"Which will be?"

"That I killed him in a fight over Hilary. I'll say I was afraid Jamie would come back to marry her."

Forsythe rubbed his chin. "Yes . . . that would be accepted. But what about Nanny Balfour?"

Dorf gave him a twisted grin. "As you remarked, I'm agile mentally. I'll tell Taylor that after I killed the dog I smothered Nanny because I've always been afraid she had suspicions about that night. Her room overlooked this area and I was afraid she might have seen me going down to the pavilion."

"Sounds weak," Miss Sanderson muttered.

Dorf shrugged. "It will serve. And I'll provide enough details to convince them I did kill Nanny."

"Such as?" Forsythe asked.

The older man didn't seem to hear him. "I didn't want to hurt Nanny. She was always kind to me. For a time after Jamie's death I was terrified that she might blurt out something about—" He broke off and muttered, "Something about Jamie and me. But then I realized she would never say anything that might tarnish her beloved boy. For years I felt safe, and it was only in the last few weeks that I started to worry again. She was failing and her mind was no longer clear. Sooner or later I knew she'd let something slip." He smiled bitterly. "With my luck it could have been to Ackerson, and he's bright enough to put two and two together and come up with the fact that Jamie never left, that he was murdered and that I might have done it. I knew it would be impossible to prove and I wasn't afraid of the law, I was afraid of Harry Moore." Dorf took a deep breath. "I knew Nanny must die."

Miss Sanderson glared at him. "So you tried to frighten her to death. Sneaking into her room and standing over her bed."

"Yes. I did that on three nights. I'd wait until the aide checked on her around one and then I'd go into her room and touch her shoulder. She'd wake up and I'd just stand there in the dark hoping . . ."

"Hoping she'd have a heart attack," the secretary muttered.

"Exactly. But it didn't work. Then that day I lunched with the other trustees and you at the home . . . well, you were there. First I found Nanny had been babbling to Falkner about an intruder in her room and then shortly afterward I heard about the dog going back time after time to Jamie's grave. I knew then I must kill both of them. That night I went in the rear door after I threw the meat to the dog, around half past eight. I figured the safest place to wait was in the nursery, and that's where I went. The door to Nanny's room was open a crack and finally I heard the aide in there, flashing her light around so she could see the patient. Then I heard the hall door close and I listened for the sound of the lift. To my shock the aide came into the nursery." He paused and his listeners pictured this man patiently waiting for hours in the darkened nursery, a specter of death among children's toys.

As Dorf continued, his voice was husky. "The aide startled me but I was able to slip into the bathroom. I hoped desperately she wasn't about to use that room. She switched on a light in the nursery and through the crack in the door I saw it was Mollie Carlyle. She sat down in Nanny's rocker and I couldn't figure out what the hell she was doing there. Then I found out. The night orderly, Tom, put in an appearance and Mollie and he started to kiss and fondle each other. Then I remembered they're engaged. They started to talk about their coming wedding and honeymoon. Then they had an argument. Mollie wants to honeymoon in Cardiff and Tom was holding out for Brighton. I thought they'd never leave but eventually they did and I heard the rumble of the descending lift, and then I went to Nanny and . . ." His voice trailed away and he averted his head. He muttered, "That will satisfy the police. Tom and Mollie will be able to testify to that conversation."

The barrister jerked his head in agreement and Dorf asked, "Will you give me your word the watch and letter will be destroyed?"

"I have a condition for that too. I'll have to read over your confession first. If I'm satisfied, then and only then will I do it."

"I understand, Forsythe. You want to be certain I don't leave loopholes."

"Precisely."

Miss Sanderson was gazing down at Dorf. "Why? Why do you want the motive for Jamie Coralund's murder concealed? For Hilary's sake?"

"You mentioned my acting ability. I don't even *like* Hilary." He rubbed a hand over his eyes. "In my entire life I've loved only two people. Jamie and my mother. My mother suffered horribly. Not only at Amos Dorf's hands but also at the hands of this town. I'm not letting them paw my mother's memory around. Now . . . can we get this over?"

The barrister turned to his secretary. "Sandy, would you run up to the home and use the phone there?"

She paused in the doorway to take one last look at Dorf.

Some murderers she had felt nothing for, some she had pitied, one she had almost admired. But this man, crumpled near the hearth where his friend and half brother had died so long ago ... She felt not one iota of pity or compassion for him. She was only anxious never to see Leroy Dorf again.

She was, partway to the home before she realized she had left her coat behind. By that time icy rain had soaked her sweater and skirt. But not even for a warm coat would she return to the pavilion. She'd wait in the home until Inspector Taylor had removed that ... that creature.

It was over two hours before Forsythe joined her. When he entered the lounge he found his secretary hunched in a chair sipping steaming coffee provided by a bewildered night nurse. As he helped Miss Sanderson into her coat, he fended off Nurse Evans's eager questions and took his secretary out to the carpark. She huddled into her coat and held his arm in a tight grip. As they reached the Rover she noticed the muscles in that arm were rigid with tension.

She asked, "Robby, what's wrong?"

"I've been wondering ... Sandy, when I threatened to hand Dorf over to Harry Moore ... I was bluffing, wasn't I?"

In his voice was a sound she hadn't heard since shortly after his mother's death. Uncertainty, confusion, fear. These emotions had looked up at her from the eyes of a small, very forlorn boy. Then she had been able to hold the child in her arms, cradle him, reassure him. The man ...

Miss Sanderson lifted her chin. "Robby, I knew your father and blimey, do I know *you*. Of course you were *bluffing*. And the bluff worked!"

Silently she admitted she never would be sure. If that bluff hadn't worked, if Dorf hadn't broken ... But her words were having the desired effect. Under her hand the muscles in his arm were relaxing. Once she had comforted the child, now she had comforted the man. The hell with too much honesty!

CHAPTER 14

Forsythe was consuming a copious lunch at the window table of the Fiddle and Bow when Harry Moore's van pulled up to the curb. Harry jumped down and gallantly helped Miss Sanderson out. Sunlight glinted from the windshield and from his secretary's freshly coiffed gray hair. Both Moore and his companion looked extremely handsome. The innkeeper was dressed in well-cut tweeds the color of tobacco, Miss Sanderson was wearing equally well-cut green tweeds.

They engaged in a long, apparently earnest conversation and then turned to the rear of the van. When Harry opened the door, Forsythe stopped with a ham roll partway to his mouth and stared. From the van bounced a golden-and-black animal that, at first glance, looked about the size of an elephant.

Muttering an oath, Forsythe sprang to his feet. Mrs. Moore slammed down a plate of salad on the table and peered past his shoulder. "Dear Lord! What has my Harry got there?"

"Your Harry and my Sandy seem to have a Great Dane. Fully grown."

"Mr. Forsythe, I'm putting my foot down! I don't mind

Harry's terriers or even his border collie but I'm not having a Great Dane in this inn!"

"I'm inclined to doubt this animal is Harry's. I have a feeling Sandy has really gone to the dogs. Here they are now. Sandy, what in the devil are you up to?"

Both his secretary and the innkeeper wore wide smiles. The Great Dane was panting and his black mask was split with what looked like a wide red smile too. Miss Sanderson selected a chair and told the dog to sit. It immediately sank back on its enormous haunches.

Mrs. Moore, her hands on her hips, glared up at her husband. "Harry Moore! This is the last straw. I've fed and tripped over dogs for years but I'm not having that . . . that cow in my inn!"

"He's not a cow," Miss Sanderson said. "He's a fully trained, two-year-old neutered male. And Robby, you and Mrs. Moore simmer down—"

"I'd like to see Aggie's face when you take that monster home with you," Forsythe said.

She raised her brows. "Keep this dog in my flat? Don't be silly. This is a replacement for Josh's Tiny."

Both Mrs. Moore and Forsythe smiled back at the dog and she said, "In that case, I take back what I said. I'll bring you pints."

As she bustled off to the bar, Forsythe sighed. "So that's where you've been all morning. Getting a dog."

"Among other things," Miss Sanderson said complacently. "Harry and I have been busy doing good deeds while you were snoring in bed—"

"I haven't been snoring in bed. I've been—"

"We were in Pendleton, Robby. Harry and I decided to beard Mr. William Perkins in his kennel—"

"I am not," Forsythe stated, "going to try to untangle that mangled metaphor."

"Abigail is a grand lady," Harry enthused. "You should have seen her swing into action. When we went into the office even my chum who works there wouldn't let us near Mr. Perkins. Seems there was a little hassle about that TV commercial they did at the home. But Abigail kind of swept all those office workers aside and—"

"You certainly helped." Miss Sanderson beamed at her ally. "Harry offered to bang the cashmere clones' heads together, and you should have seen Ted and Larry and Doug scurry!"

Forsythe held up a hand. "Just what was your purpose in bearding the manufacturer of Perky Puppy Puffs in his kennel?"

Harry pulled out his battered cigar case. "Wasn't much like a kennel, Robert. Mr. Perkins has got a big fancy office. Lots of polished wood and a desk big enough to dance on. Scads of dog pictures around and he had two of his dogs in the office. One was a black Labrador I'd sure like to own and the other—"

"Will you answer my question?" Forsythe demanded.

"Patience, Robby." Miss Sanderson picked up the stein Mrs. Moore had just deposited and took a long swig. "The purpose of our visit was to make Mr. Perkins cough up the money to look after the dogs at the home. Poopsie and the one Harry and I were getting for Josh. Harry and I have renamed this one. The breeder called him Brutus but that's a dumb name. So—" She stroked the huge head and the Great Dane gave her an appreciative leer. "We are calling him Tinkle."

Forsythe grinned. "That's a dumb name too."

"Any successor to Tiny must be called Tinkle. Where was I?"

"Forcing Mr. Perkins to cough up cash."

"As I reminded him, he had started this whole business and it's his responsibility. Harry told him about Poopsie and Tiny and how much they've done for Josh Pitts and Maggie."

"He turned out to be a grand old gentleman," Harry

said. "Seems he blames the little problem about filming on those idiots in publicity. Said Ted and Doug and
Larry don't even *like* dogs. By the time I got done Mr.
Perkins's eyes were kind of watery and he said he knew
how Maggie and Josh must feel. So he told us to get
another Great Dane for Josh, and not only would he
pay for it but see money is provided for the dogs' keep
and to pay a boy to exercise them. Ended up with us
drinking his brandy and talking about dogs. Mr. Perkins told us to be sure and come back to see him again.
Fine chap!"

"He was very decent," Miss Sanderson agreed. "Now,
Robby, what did *you* do with your morning?"

"Compared with your escapades, it was on the dull side.
First I conferred with Inspector Taylor, then I read Dorf's
confession." Forsythe looked at his secretary. "Then I
made a brief stop at the library."

"And you did what Dorf wanted?" Miss Sanderson
asked.

He patted a pocket. "I kept my part of the bargain."

Ruddy color flooded Harry's broad face. "What bargain?"

Forsythe shrugged. "Nothing that has any bearing on
the trial."

"Speaking of trial, Robert, it's been over a week since
that swine owned up to killing Nanny and Jamie. Awful
slow, isn't it?"

Forsythe gazed out through the window. "The mills of
justice," he said softly, "like that of the gods grind slowly
but exceedingly fine."

"They better," the innkeeper said grimly. "He better pay.
What kind of sentence do you figure he'll get?"

"A long one. Not for James Coralund's death. Dorf in-
sists that was an accident and it probably was. But Nanny's
murder was definitely premeditated, and I should imagine
the judge will throw the book at Dorf for that."

"If he doesn't they should throw out that book. Even hanging's too good for that—"

"Robby," Miss Sanderson interrupted. "Do you know what Harry told me on the drive to Pendleton? He's handed in his resignation as a trustee."

"Congratulations!" Forsythe shook hands with the older man. "Sounds like a good move. You'll be able to devote more time to your business."

"And to my Sally." Harry raised the big hand Forsythe had just released and waved at his wife. She waved back. Her face flushed with warm color and when she smiled there was a trace of the radiance that had made her so attractive as a bride. Harry added, "Hilary's Gang is finally broken up and thank God for that. I understand Sean Ackerson is selling his business and—"

"Taking off to warmer climes," Forsythe said dryly.

"He's talking about the south of France. Buying a villa there."

Draining her stein, Miss Sanderson said, "Guess who the new trustees are."

"First tell me if Miss Coralund is remaining on the board."

"Of course she is, Robby. Hilary would never give that position up."

"My first guess would be Ben Falkner, M.D."

"Right you are." The innkeeper's eyes glinted with admiration. "Robert, you really are a detective."

"Bet your boots he is," Miss Sanderson said smugly. "And the vicar and Mrs. Parker have volunteered to take the other two vacancies."

"Great." Forsythe consulted his watch. "Look at the time. I must head for home. Sandy, you'll be back later today?"

She shook her head. "Tomorrow. I have to take this dog up to the home and I want to spend some time with Maggie and Josh. When you get back to London would you give Aggie a ring? Tell her I'll be home by dinnertime tomorrow."

He rose and picked up his Burberry. "Any other messages for her?"

Miss Sanderson stood up. "Tell Aggie my cold is better and I'm feeling fine. And . . . tell her I've missed her."

"Good girl. Walk me to my car?"

"Certainly. Come along, Tinkle, I'm taking you to meet your new master. Heel, boy."

The dog obediently heeled and Harry said, "Josh is sure going to be happy." He handed her a ring of keys. "Better take the van. Be hard to fit that big boy into your MG."

"Good thinking." Miss Sanderson waited while Forsythe said good-bye. He received a thump on the shoulder from Harry and a peck on the cheek from Mrs. Moore.

As they stepped out of the inn, Forsythe sneezed and reached for a handkerchief. "Ah," his secretary said. "You're getting my cold."

"I'm afraid so."

"Try raw garlic sprinkled with salt. It's supposed to work miracles." She led the Great Dane to the van, swung open the door, and commanded, "In, Tinkle."

Tinkle docilely hopped in and she shut the door. Turning, she winked at Forsythe. "Have to run now, Robby. Got to see a man about a dog."

He laughed and called, "Awesome!"

"Do you always have to have the last word?"

"Yes," Robert Forsythe said.